DARKNESS LOOMS: JACK FACES WAR

ALSO BY MARK GREATHOUSE

The Frontier Chronicles

Perilous Trails: Jack's Adventure Begins

Wyoming Calls: Jack's Risky Quest

Longhorns North: Jack's Great Trail Drive

Warpath: Jack's Faith is Tested

Hunter Vs. Hunted: Jack's Great Frontier Challenge

Freedom Drovers: Jack's Awesome Crusade

A Poison Spreads: Jack Seeks the Antidote

The Tumbleweed Sagas

Nueces Justice

Nueces Reprise

Nueces Deceit

Nueces Blood

Nueces Grit

Nueces Truth

Nueces Legend

Lone Star Vigilante

DARKNESS LOOMS: JACK FACES WAR

THE FRONTIER CHRONICLES
BOOK 8

MARK GREATHOUSE

WISE WOLF
BOOKS

Darkness Looms: Jack Faces War
Paperback Edition
Copyright © 2025 by Mark Greathouse

WISE WOLF BOOKS
An Imprint of Wolfpack Publishing
1707 E. Diana Street
Tampa, FL 33610

wisewolfbooks.com

All rights reserved. No part of this book may be reproduced in any form
or by any electronic or mechanical means, including information
storage and retrieval systems, without express written permission from
the publisher, except for the use of brief quotations in reviews. Any use
of this publication to train generative artificial intelligence (AI)
technologies is expressly prohibited.

This book is a work of fiction. References to historical events, real
people, or real places are used fictitiously. Any similarity to real
persons, living or dead, is purely coincidental and not intended by the
author.

Paperback ISBN 978-1-965596-45-6
eBook ISBN 978-1-965596-44-9
LCCN 2025940372

Dedicated with love to my wife Carolyn, our two sons Mike and Matt, and the memory of my father John F. (Jack) Greathouse

"There is a time for everything, and a season for every activity under the heavens:

a time to love and a time to hate, a time for war and a time for peace."

ECCLESIASTES 3:1 & 8

"The hope of the righteous is joy, but the expectation of the wicked comes to nothing.

The way of the Lord is a stronghold for the honorable, but destruction awaits the malicious.

The righteous will never be shaken, but the wicked will not remain on the earth.

The mouth of the righteous produces wisdom, but a perverse tongue will be cut out."

PROVERBS 10:28-31

JACK'S UNDERGROUND RAILROAD

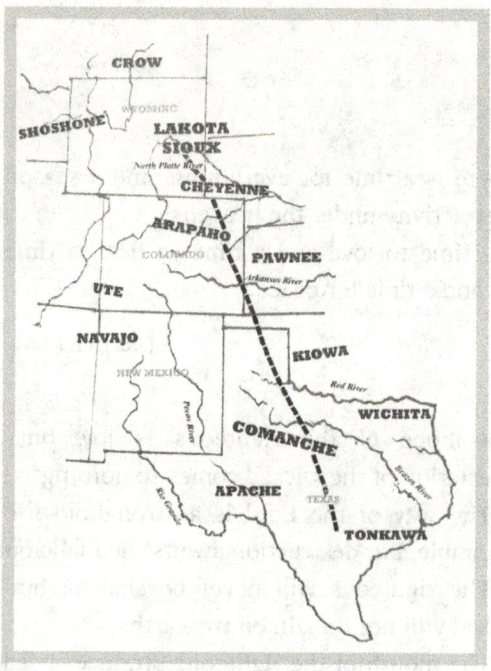

Route used by Jack and Spirit Talker in sneaking escaped slaves northward from Texas to Wyoming. It featured challenging landscapes and many tribes known to be hostile. Notably, it followed the Great Western Trail eventually used for great cattle drives. (Map by Mark Greathouse)

YOU ARE INVITED

Dear Reader,

If you've read *Perilous Trails* and the follow-on Frontier Chronicles series, it's likely my story has fully grabbed you. This eighth part of my tale carries my story through the War Between the States and on to 1872. You recall that back in 1855, I had been thrown alone and vulnerable onto the vast Comancheria, made dangerous by the predations against White settlers by Comanche and Kiowa. I am now twenty years old. I've journeyed four times to Wyoming, first exploring the trail northward, twice driving herds of longhorns to my friend George Freeman's ranch on the North Platte, and once escaping threats to my family. Hostilities between Whites and Indians had exploded. But the poison of slavery spreading throughout the nation had erupted in a great war. Me and my family become truly tested.

Darkness Looms: Jack Faces War shares the further testing of my courage, faith, endurance, pure grit, and my mission. The Indians call me *Pohya Isa* or *Walks With Wolves*. My adventures sure have taught me a ton of life lessons. Do keep in mind that my story incorporates history not found in most school history books. This book relates my tale as driven by fate and guided by God.

I have met up with plenty of Indians, especially Comanche and Lakota Sioux, so you'll find me using some of their language throughout *Darkness Looms*. I have provided a handy glossary of Comanche and Lakota words toward the back of this book.

I'm a Christian, but I have tried to grasp the Comanche and Lakota religions to better understand them. The Indian religion is based upon what is referred to as animism, in which every common natural item, from fish and animals to plants, trees, waterways, and mountains, were believed to have souls or spirits. The spirits and traditions connected with them guided the Comanche and Lakota. Their passion for their spirits no doubt gave them their fearlessness as fed by the belief that they were protected in everything they did. Would they kill to defend their beliefs? Theirs was not a religion of love and forgiveness.

Could Indians like the Comanche or Lakota become Christians? My story in Darkness Looms continues my evolution at the intersection of faith and culture. It was like Saint Patrick's conversion of the Irish to Christianity by folding many of their less-offensive heathen rites into the Catholic faith. Would this work with the Indians? Well, it's part of the story I'm sharing with y'all.

As you follow my adventures, ask yourself whether you might be up to meeting the challenges I take on. Dangers? Privations? Hmmm. How might you have fared? Through it all, I first relied on the teachings from my family, then went on to learn from the raw and risky experiences I faced. I learned to trust in instincts forged from my biblical lessons.

To be straight here, I had no idea that my story was going to fill multiple volumes until I began to write it all down. I invite you to follow my adventures on America's western frontier.

Kindest regards,

John *Jack* O'Toole

THE CAST

Jack O'Toole—*Twenty-year-old son of Joseph and Kate O'Toole. He strives to carve a life from the Texas frontier on the easternmost reaches of the Comancheria. Earned Comanche name Pohya Isa, Walks With Wolves.*

Mukwooru (aka, Spirit Talker)—*Twenty-year-old son of a Penateka Comanche chief camped within the heart of the Comancheria. The warrior name bestowed upon teen Wild Horse in recognition of his apparent connection with Taa Narumi —the Comanche Great Father—whom they confused with God.*

Blue Flower—*Young sister to Spirit Talker and daughter to Buffalo Hump, she's married to Jack. They have four young children, George, Isa, Peter, and Nadua.*

George Freeman—*A Black cowboy driving cattle north, later an Army scout. He establishes a ranch on the North Platte River in Wyoming.*

Running Waters—*George Freeman's Pawnee wife.*

Kate—*Jack's sixteen-year-old sister now married to Will Smith.*

Buck—*Jack's thirteen-year-old brother.*

Isaac Fisher—*An Amish farmer from Pennsylvania seeking new opportunity on the frontier.*

Sarah Fisher—*Isaac Fisher's wife and mother to baby son named Jack.*

Topsannah (aka, Prairie Flower)—*Young Comanche girl captured and enslaved by Arapaho. Lived on George Freeman's ranch. Marries Spirit Talker.*

Sam Collins—*Owner of the Circle C Ranch located near Jack's spread.*

Hank Johnson—*Cowhand on Collins's Circle C Ranch.*

Juan Perez—*Creative, hard-nosed Mexican cook on Jack's trail drive.*

Shorty McBride—*Drover on Jack's Crusade who lives up to his nickname.*

Willard *Will* Smith—*First hired hand on the Rising Cross Ranch. He marries Kate O'Toole.*

Stella Klappenbach—*August Klappenbach's wife.*

Hardy Sullivan—*Grizzled Texas Ranger who becomes friends with Jack and finds God.*

William McGregor—*A Scottish immigrant who serves as blacksmith and pastor in Austin, TX.*

Colleen McGregor—*William McGregor's wife.*

Zeb (Zebadiah)—*A wolf that Jack believes is a gift from God. They develop an ever-closer bond as the Frontier Chronicles evolve.*

Reginald Wilson IV—*Legacy nephew of Sarah Fisher sent west to learn how to be a man.*

Cutter Kincaid—*Elfin hermit-like survivor of life who helps abolitionists.*

Sheesha—*Escaped woman slave who seeks to become a cowpoke. Frederick's close friend.*

Colt Crockett—*Wrangler for Sam Collins's Circle C Ranch and friend to Jack O'Toole.*

Samuel—*Indentured servant whom Jack rescues from a*

maniacal plantation owner. He's part Cherokee, Black, and White.

Galt Smathers—*Notorious killer who poses a threat to Jack.*

Digger Brown & Tex Waltrip—*Revenge-seeking friends of Galt Smathers.*

Rowdy Sikes—*Leader of vigilantes based near Rising Cross Ranch and later Confederate officer.*

Virgil Tubbs—*Representative of the post-war reconstruction government.*

Benito *Booger* Salido—*Mexican bandit who seizes on Texans post-war vulnerabilities to rustle cattle.*

Taabe—*Offspring of Zebediah*

HISTORICAL CHARACTERS

Sam Houston—*Leader of Texas independence, first president of Texas, leads them to statehood, serves as governor and US Senator.*

Potsunakwahipu (aka, Buffalo Hump)—*War chief of the Penateka Comanche, the uthernmost band of the Comanche people in the Comancheria. In the famous Council House Fight of 1840, he led roughly a thousand Comanche across Texas to the Gulf Coast where theyransacked Victoria and burned Linnville.*

Tasunke Witko (aka, Crazy Horse)—Future chief of Oglala Lakota of the Sioux Nation. He is *about 19 years old at the time of this story, but already gaining attention of tribal leaders. He will go on to lead the massacre of General Custer's troops at Little Big Horn (aka, Greasy Grass) in 1876.*

Tatanka Iyotake (aka, Sitting Bull)—Chief and medicine man of the Hunkpapa band of Lakota *Sioux.*

August Klappenbach—*Early settler of Bandera, TX and owner of the first general store and post office.*

Thomas Twiss—*Indian agent assigned to Fort Laramie region.*

John Salmon *Rip* Ford—*Texas Ranger, doctor, lawyer,*

journalist, newspaper owner, legislator, and eventual Confederate colonel.

Quanah Parker—*Eventual chief of the Quahadi band of the Comanche nation. Son of Comanche Chief Peta Nocona and White captive Cynthia Ann Parker.*

Ed Maier—*Sheriff of Gillespie County, Texas.*

William Quantrill—*Confederate Rebel leader who wreaks havoc throughout Kansas.*

DARKNESS LOOMS: JACK FACES WAR

PROLOGUE

I HAD JUST ROUNDED the trail. The full realization of whom I was seeing didn't strike me right away, given the condition of the two bodies hanging high from a live oak branch. Buck and Hardy pulled up beside me with Shorty driving the wagon just moments later. They were stunned into silence. The scene was horrific.

I released a scream like no other the world could ever possibly have known. My body was racked with great sobs of grief, then swept with anger. What demon could have done this deed?

Nudging Big Red forward and drawing my Bowie knife, I cut the ropes. The bodies had been so decimated by scavengers that they nearly fell apart on impact. As it was, I barely recognized the escaped slave Sheesha and her new husband, Samuel. A couple of days hanging from the tree, coupled with the tortures they'd endured, took their toll. The scavengers could have cared less and resented our intrusion.

Zeb chased away a couple of lurking coyotes while the buzzards squawked their displeasure.

I slid from Big Red and kneeled beside the bodies. How could this have happened? Who did it? Why? I knew all the answers save the who. It had likely been slave catchers. But why had they not sought the bounty on Sheesha?

Shorty leaped from the wagon with a shovel in hand and began digging. Buck grabbed a couple of blankets and pitched in to help.

I struggled to overcome my emotions, to gather my reasoning. Anger and desire for vengeance loomed large, as I grappled with the faith my pa had instilled in me as a boy, and I had to turn to when Comanche massacred my family. I shook my head vigorously, as if to chase the vitriol from brain. I needed to regain control of myself and apply the tracking skills I'd learned from Spirit Talker. There had to be some sign of what had happened. Was there a struggle? What happened to their horses and supplies?

The emotions—the passions—surrounding slavery were all-too-real. And it seemed that violence was increasing. I sensed that a great darkness loomed, the foreboding shadow of a great conflict to come.

ONE
CLUES

WE EASED the bodies into the shallow grave. It seemed fitting that husband and wife be buried together. I said a prayer, and Hardy planted a crudely-fashioned cross at the head with Sheesha's and Samuel's names carved into it.

I guess it might seem a tad macabre, but I gathered up the two hangman's nooses and cleaned them as best I could. I said a short prayer as I wrapped them in a piece of leather and stuffed them in my saddlebag. I felt some sense that whomever had done this deed, should eventually wear the nooses.

With that, I directed Shorty, Buck, and Hardy to stay with the wagon while I began a deep scouting of the site. I felt confident that there had to be clues. Who might have been aware of the couple's departure from Rising Cross Ranch? I could think of no one that didn't hold my absolute trust. This was either random or the work of someone spying on our activities. Sheesha and Samuel had been on their way to enjoying the opportunities of freedom, and they'd been robbed of it in a most heinous manner. From the tree where they'd met their final fate, I began carefully treading the ground in ever greater circles. There had to be clues. There were a few feathers spread about, as though whoever perpetrated this ugly deed sought to place blame on Indians. Were it not so somber an occasion, it might have brought a laugh.

I did find the hoofprints of Samuel's horse nearly lost in the prints of as many as a dozen shod horses. His horse's hoofprints were distinctive, as they were wider than most. Shod cayuses? They sure weren't Indian ponies. The tracks led off to the northwest toward Fredericksburg. I had walked the circle to better than a hundred feet radius, when I came upon a surprising clue. It was surprising in that it had been left behind. How on earth does anyone snap a Bowie knife in two? Hidden under the cactus before me lay the shiny silver blade. Could it have belonged to the murderers? There were no signs of rust, so it had found its way beneath the cactus recently. I added it to my saddlebag. I could see that Shorty, Hardy, and Buck were growing impatient. I had to admit that the place had an aura of creepiness about it. I was about to quit, when a few items discarded from Sheesha's and Samuel's possessions were piled behind a tree. They didn't amount to much, but I tossed them in the wagon anyway.

I glanced around at the somber faces before me and sighed resignedly. "Let's get back on the trail." In my mind, and despite my Christian teachings, I couldn't help but think that some folks might be wanting to size up grave space. Feelings of hurt, anger, sadness, and more filled my being.

———

AS WE WENDED our way up the Pinta Trail, I caught a glimpse now and then of the hoofprints of Samuel's horse along with the others. I felt that those prints would likely accompany us all the way to Fredericksburg. After no more than a dozen miles, all but three horses parted company and headed south. Samuel's mount and the two others remained on the Pinta Trail.

Upon reaching the Pedernales River, we were alerted to approaching visitors by the sound of shod horses and jingles of sabers. A cavalry patrol appeared with a young lieutenant in the lead. He brought the patrol to a halt but a few yards from us. "Who goes?" he asked in a military spit and polish manner.

I had been riding in front of our caravan at the time and reined in Big Red. Zeb dutifully pulled alongside. "Just heading to Fredericksburg for supplies," I responded. "My name's Jack O'Toole. To who am I speaking?"

I had the temerity to have challenged the all-too-obviously wet-behind-the-ears officer. Or, at least, he took it that way.

"I'm Lieutenant Abraham Button out of Camp Leona," he responded, with a squinty-eyed look as he raised his hand to bring his company to a halt. He cast a suspicious eye at Zeb. It seemed most folks were rather taken aback to encounter a tamed wolf.

I could see that the troops were a roughshod, ragtag mess. Only eleven remained from what was likely twice that number. They were a long way from Camp Leona and appeared to have engaged enemies a time or two. Two troopers' arms were in slings. Judging from three empty-saddled horses, I reckoned they'd mostly been lucky to have escaped with their scalps attached.

"You're a long way from Uvalde, Lieutenant," I observed as respectfully as I could muster.

The lieutenant lifted his cover and wiped beads of sweat from his forehead. "Been chasing Kiowa," he informed us.

I suppressed a knowing grin. "Pardon, but it seems they found you." I scanned the company. "Y'all seem to have lost your packhorses. We'd be happy to share some of our food and water."

The lieutenant sighed resignedly. The eleven mounted troopers were awaiting his decision to accept our offer. "Troop at ease. Fall out," he directed. The troopers dismounted, gathered at our wagon, and accepted food about as fast as Buck could hand it out. They availed themselves of water, as well.

"I'm much obliged, Mr. O'Toole," said Button. The lieutenant had by now begun to realize that he'd happened upon travelers experienced with the ways of the frontier. "Your necklace? Did you?"

"Kill the bear? Afraid so," I answered humbly.

"Mind if we accompany you to Fredericksburg?" Button asked.

I nodded. "Just keep an eye on our backtrail. I have some friends among the Kiowa, but they aren't always reliable," I said with a knowing wink.

Hunger and thirst sated, the troopers mounted up, and we resumed our journey.

TWO
CONFRONTATION

GIVEN the condition of Button's men, we journeyed on through a starlit night. We arrived at Fredericksburg at first light. Button expressed his gratitude and went off to care for his troopers. I reckoned to visit the McGregors and then resupply at Reggie Wilson's store.

I led us up the main street and reined in Big Red at McGregor's shop. There was the sign I loved, greeting us.

WILLIAM MCGREGOR
Smithy and Preacher
Sins & Iron Hammered Out Here

SHORTY STAYED WITH THE WAGON, while Buck, Hardy, and I headed into the shop. Will McGregor's back was to us, and he was hammering away on a red-hot branding iron. Sparks shot from the anvil's surface with each mighty stroke.

"William McGregor," I announced.

McGregor dropped the branding iron and spun

around with his hammer poised on high and ready to strike. He stared at me a split-second and then relaxed with a broad smile. "Dang, Jack O'Toole, I coulda kilt yuh!"

"You remember Hardy and Buck here. Shorty's back in the wagon. We come to Fredericksburg for supplies."

"Look on yer face says yuh met some trouble," observed McGregor.

"You could say that," I responded with considerable understatement.

"Yer wagon's all right. Invite Shorty an' we'll have some coffee. Yuh kin tell me 'bout it."

We gathered around the battered old table in McGregor's kitchen while Stella poured hot coffee. I don't believe in long, heavily embellished tales, so it didn't take long to fill Will in on all that happened during our journey to Fredericksburg.

While the engagement between the troopers and Kiowa was concerning, McGregor was nearly as distraught as me about Sheesha and Samuel. The horror of what had befallen them was mind-numbing. How could a human unleash such evils upon another human? How could skin color possibly matter? We all bled red. "Sorry, Jack. May the Lord bring peace to yer soul over this. Y'all are welcome to spend the night here."

"Much obliged, Will. We do need to head up yonder to Reggie's store to gather supplies."

McGregor gave me a deadly serious look. "You've gotta out last 'em, lad."

"How is Blue Feather?" asked Stella.

"Ah, thanks for asking. We have a fourth baby due in about three months or thereabouts. Isa and George are growing like prairie grass during rainy season and Peter is trying to walk." I turned to McGregor. "Rising Cross is growing. We've got some hundred and sixty thousand acres now and livestock is multiplying like crazed rabbits."

"But?" queried McGregor.

"The day may come when we must leave. I feel in my bones that big trouble is ahead, Will. It's like a darkness looming on the horizon," I lamented.

We decided to visit Reggie's store, spend the night with the McGregors, and hit the trail home in the morning.

————

WE LEFT our cayuses with McGregor and drove the wagon up the street to Reggie's store. As Shorty reined in the team, I glanced past him. Samuel's horse stood across the street with reins tied at a hitching rail in front of what appeared to be some sort of saloon. The saddle was the one we gave to Samuel, so there was no mistaking the horse and tack.

"Shorty, do you see that?" I said, slipping from Big Red's back.

"Whatcha thinkin', boss?" responded Shorty.

Hardy nonchalantly rode over to the cayuse, then eased his horse back to the wagon. "It's sportin' our Rising Cross brand," he noted.

I sighed. The anger from discovering the bodies of Sheesha and Samuel threatened to well up in me. "Lord help me," I whispered. Zeb nudged me with his muzzle as if to calm me. My mind had begun to churn chaotically, but Zeb's simple act worked. "Shorty, you go about our business of purchasing supplies from Reggie. Buck, fetch the sheriff. Hardy and I are going to see who rode that bronc into town."

Hardy and I hitched our horses and cautiously walked across the street to the saloon. There were five other horses hitched along with the one we'd given to Samuel. We paused at the horse and gave the gelding a gentle pat before climbing the two steps up to the plank boardwalk. We stepped through the doorway and paused to let our eyes become accustomed to the dimness inside. The saloon reeked of sweat, booze, and leather. It offered a sharp contrast to the clear, sunny day. There were five tables, and three were occupied by a nondescript clientele of cowboys. There were eight in all.

Hardy headed for an empty table in the back corner, while I strode over to the bar. Now, I am not a drinking man but I reckoned this was one time it might be a good idea to act like one.

The barkeep eased over. "What'll you gents be havin'?"

"Beer," I responded. A glance around the room as I awaited the beer caused me to realize that all eyes were on me. Okay, I'm a big man and wearing buckskins. It wasn't exactly what would be deemed cowboy attire. The bear claw necklace was an attention-getter. Then, it struck me that the eyes were looking at Zeb. It wasn't every day that a man with a wolf strode into the saloon. I smiled, as I hefted the two beers and headed to where Hardy sat. Zeb padded along behind me. The eyes in the saloon followed us.

Before sitting, I turned to face the men. "Anyone here happen to know who's riding that roan gelding out front?"

"Who wants to know?" came a growl from a couple of tables away.

"Just asking," I replied.

"It's my hoss. You got a problem with that?"

"My name is Jack O'Toole. I own Rising Cross Ranch east of here. That cayuse is bearing my brand. Do you have a bill of sale?"

The now disgruntled hombre stood. "I traded for it."

"Do you have a name? It'd be polite to know who I'm talking with," I said firmly.

"Galt Smathers. What's it to you?" came the response. "You accusing me of something?" He sat by himself. From what I could see, he wore a dark gray shirt and a flat, broad-brimmed hat. A bushy handlebar mustache graced his upper lip, and a scar weaved its way down the left side of his face.

"Traded for him, you say? Where might that have taken place?"

Hardy slipped his Colt from its holster and held it under the edge of the table and at the ready.

Smathers was momentarily disconcerted as he struggled with a sensical answer. "Er...Bandera. Yep. Traded for it in Bandera," he finally blurted.

"What if I told you that bronc has never been near Bandera?" I challenged him.

A couple of the cowboys left their tables and scurried out of the saloon. The situation had begun to heat up a tad.

"You calling me a liar?" said Smathers.

"Just saying your story isn't holding together. Who did you trade with?"

Smathers stood. His right hand hovered over the revolver on his hip. "That's none of your business."

Despite having Hardy as backup, I sure wasn't up to having some sort of shoot-'em-up. My mind raced. Zeb's ears were pricked up, and he stood ready for action.

Smathers looked at Zeb, and a touch of fear entered his eyes.

"I found the man who owned that cayuse hanging by a rope along the Pinta Trail a couple of days back. Tell me again how you came by it." I was digging in hard.

Smathers squirmed a bit. His eyes went from me to Zeb and back. It was becoming obvious that despite all his blather about trading for the horse, he was having serious second thoughts about taking us on. "Look…er… I'm not lookin' for trouble. The Nigra and breed had it coming."

The anger swelled within me. Smathers had been with the gang that waylaid and murdered Sheesha and Samuel. Should I yield to my baser instincts and kill the murderer here and now? "The man sitting behind me is a retired Texas Ranger and has a gun leveled on your midsection. I rode with Captain Rip Ford and have fought far tougher hombres than you. One of my men has gone to find the sheriff." I let that sink in. "You would do well to unfasten your gun belt and ease the rig onto the table. The alternative won't be pretty."

Smathers's eyes flitted nervously. His fingers hovered over his gun and twitched as he thought out his situation. The noise of the sheriff climbing onto the boardwalk in front of the saloon helped him decide. "I ain't dying today," he finally said decisively and began unbuckling his gun belt.

"Why did y'all do it?" I asked.

Smathers gave an insolent shrug.

"This the man?" asked Sheriff Ed Maier with a questioning look at me.

"Horse thieving and possibly murder, Sheriff," I stated unequivocably.

"I'm no murderer!" declared Smathers. "Negras and breeds don't count!"

The outlaw had just admitted to murder, but his

confession hadn't sunk in with Maier. "He's riding a horse with my brand. I gifted the horse just a few days back to a man named Samuel. This man Smathers has no proof of sale or trade with Samuel," I said, reckoning that I could have him locked up for horse thieving if not murder.

Maier gave me a helpless sort of look. "Was this Samuel a White man?"

"Partly," I admitted.

The sheriff shook his head. "Can't arrest him," he stated flatly.

In a state where Blacks, Indians, and Mexicans weren't counted as part of the population, I wasn't surprised. For me to insist on Smathers's arrest would not likely go well for me or my men. I fought to contain my frustration.

Smathers gave me a *you-can-go-to-hell* look with a smirk that screamed out for my fist.

Hardy arose and holstered his gun. "I'm puttin' the word out to my Texas Ranger friends, Smathers. You best be watchin' yer backtrail," he said and stalked out the front door with me, Buck, and Zeb following.

I did give the sheriff a nasty look on the way out. It was deserving of a man with no spine for delivering justice.

We crossed the street and helped Shorty load the final batch of supplies in the wagon. I watched with seething anger as Smathers mounted Samuel's horse, looked my way, still wearing that smirk, and rode off.

The sheriff emerged. He glanced over at us sheepishly, shrugged, and beat his feet up the street.

———

IT WAS a relief to get back to the McGregor shop. We stored the wagon in his shed and settled down for dinner and good conversation around the hearth. Naturally, we related our encounter with Smathers.

"I know of him, Jack," offered McGregor. "Nasty, that one," he assured me.

"A bad one, heh?" I responded.

"Worse than bad. Lucky the sheriff was around or there'd ah been shootin'." He gave a dismayed head-shake. "Word has it, the man's kilt nigh twenty, maybe more."

It seemed that the outcome of my run-in with Smathers might not have ended well, if Sheriff Maier hadn't been found. The sheriff quite clearly had a problem with Black folks and Indians, but it didn't excuse his letting Smathers free. At the very least, he should have arrested him for horse stealing. "I'm not sure which is worse, the slavery problem or the Indian problem," I ventured. It seemed that ethics—the moral principles governing folks' behavior—was in play here and there wasn't nearly enough being applied. Why couldn't folks simply care about each other? Christ preached love, but far too many ignored His preaching.

"What do you figure we do?" asked Buck.

"Well, we do need to return to Rising Cross." I took a long sip of the coffee Colleen had served us. I looked out the window. "I've got a feeling creeping up my spine that we haven't heard the last of Galt Smathers."

Zeb padded on over and licked my hand.

"We'd best head out in the morning."

———

"YOU SEE THAT, HARDY?" My jaw dropped, as I pointed ahead of us along the south bank of the Pedernales River. He and I were riding point a couple of hundred yards in front of the wagon driven by Buck and Shorty. I reined in.

"What's that!" exclaimed Hardy.

"It's one of those camels like the ones they were messing with down at Camp Verde near Bandera." I wondered what it was doing so far from the camp.

"Do yuh ride'em or eat'em?" Hardy wondered aloud.

"It's not a very pretty beast. I sure don't aim to ride one and I'm not sure they're decent eating."

Hardy smiled mischievously. We'd been uptight since dealing with Sheesha and Samuel and then encountering Smathers. "I think one of us gotta ride thet thing."

While we sat our saddles and pondered his proposition, the wagon caught up to us.

I looked at Hardy, and he returned my gaze. We smiled.

"Hey, Buck! We bet yuh can't ride thet thing," challenged Hardy.

Meanwhile, I nudged Big Red along gently until we were close to the camel. I noted that it bore a US Army brand. It also wore the remains of a halter, so I dismounted and eased over while talking gently to the ungainly beast.

The camel gave me a suspicious look but permitted me to grasp the halter. I gently motioned to Buck to come over.

Buck's gaze was every bit as suspicious as the camel's.

"Think you can ride him, brother?" I hoped that it had been saddlebroken.

Poor Buck. He was between a rock and a hard place. Three sets of eyeballs were riveted in on him and daring him to ride. Buck eased his horse alongside the camel and managed to climb aboard the camel's back.

That camel took off like it'd been shot from a cannon. We busted our bellies laughing, while Buck did all he could to hang on for dear life.

All was going daringly well until the beast ran under a branch, and Buck failed to duck. There was a sickening thud, as the tree branch caught him chest-high. He dropped to the ground like a sack of potatoes.

We ran to Buck's side. He was out cold and was going to have a whale of a bruise when he came to. The camel? It faded from sight.

Buck was just beginning to come around, as we laid him on top of the supplies in the wagon. He gave me a groggy-eyed look, then passed out.

Shorty, Hardy, and I had all we could handle suppressing laughs from our dastardly deed.

———

WELL, Buck finally came around. His chest was sore as all get out but he forgave us. We reached the Pinta Trail and turned southward. We'd managed to negotiate the trail going north with the wagon so we reckoned to be able to handle the journey south.

We had traveled a couple of hours along the trail, and I was riding point when it happened. Big Red and I followed a bend in the trail that momentarily placed us out of sight of the wagon. I had my ears on alert as an eerie silence struck me. I glanced down at Zeb, and he was sniffing the air. Big Red's ears pricked up and his nostrils flared. Too late! An explosion shattered the air. My last conscious feeling was of being lifted from my saddle by whatever hit me. I was oblivious to being sprawled flat on my back behind Big Red. Blood seeped from a bullet hole in my left shoulder. My senses returned for a moment, then all went black. The last thing I recalled hearing were the hoofbeats of Hardy's and Buck's horses heading toward me.

THREE
RACE FOR LIFE

I AWAKENED IN MY BED. I glanced around the room to confirm. Yep, it was my bed. I had no idea how I'd gotten here. Moments later, I heard the soft patter of feet, and Blue Flower appeared in the doorway.

"Jack awake," she cooed with a relieved smile.

My head spun a little, as I tried to sit up, then fell back.

"Jack shot. Much blood. Fear *kooitu*." She stroked my forehead.

What had she said? I'd almost died?

"Shorty, Hardy, Buck bring Jack home in wagon." She sat beside me. "Blue Flower afraid. Happy Jack live."

"Who shot me?"

Blue Flower shrugged. "Zeb chase. Zeb no come home."

I desperately wanted to get up, but my body wouldn't cooperate.

She stroked my face. "Jack rest."

So, I'd been shot, bushwhacked I figured. My groggy brain tried to work out who might have done such a thing. I guess I had been in a sort of race for life—mine. And where was Zeb? Zeb? Zeb? I fell asleep.

———

THE OAK BENCH on the gallery made for hard seating, but Blue Flower had placed a blanket under me. I sat there with my left arm in a sling and wielded a coffee cup in my right hand. Shorty stood leaning against the gallery post while Hardy and Buck sat on another bench nearby.

"We'd just started trekking down the Pinta Trail, boss. Shot come oughta nowhere. Of a sudden, you be lyin' on the trail. Heard a hoss ridin' away. Zeb took off after it." Shorty paused to let the story sink in. I'd heard it once already, but asked them here to hear it again. "You be bleedin' bad. We stopped the bleedin' best we could an' lay yuh in the wagon. Got back here quick as we could."

"No idea who the bushwhacker was?"

The three shook their heads.

"Zeb hasn't returned?"

Again, three heads shook.

Blue Flower adjusted the pillow behind my head and sat beside me.

Buck looked at Shorty and Hardy for approval. They nodded affirmatively. "I'm thinking it was that Smathers fellow."

I chewed on that a moment.

"He wasn't happy about us trying to jail him for murder and horse stealing," added Buck.

"Makes sense," contributed Hardy. "My Texas Ranger bones would suspect him first."

I had to agree. Smathers was surely a nasty-enough

customer to bushwhack me. "Guess we have to go after him."

"You ain't goin' anywhere, boss," advised Shorty. "Only been a week since you were shot. You have healing to do."

"Where's Zeb?" I asked.

The three shrugged.

As if on queue, two sad blue eyes framed by a shaggy face emerged at the end of the gallery. Zeb limped onto the boards and collapsed. Muddied and bloodied, he was barely breathing. Blue Flower rushed over. "Warm water," she called. "Get him inside!"

A long, raw gash ran along Zeb's side. He'd lost a lot of blood. I marveled that he'd made it home. There was dried blood around his jaws, leading me to believe that he might have wounded whoever he'd met. Shorty and Buck lifted him gently and brought him inside. Zeb offered no protest, as they placed him on the kitchen table. I managed to follow and sit close enough to gently stroke Zeb's mane.

Blue Flower bathed the gaping wound and went to work stitching it together. Zeb seemed to sense that he was in good hands. He never flinched. She then applied a Comanche healing poultice. Only time would tell how effective it would be.

Now, I had time to think on how to pursue Galt Smathers. I tried to get inside his evil mind. Where would a man like him go? What had happened in his life to lead him down the path he'd chosen? Had he ever been loved? Had he ever loved? Not likely. What had influenced the path he'd taken? Perhaps the most important question was whether he thought that he'd killed me? I also wondered whether Zeb had wounded him.

———

A COUPLE OF WEEKS PASSED, and I managed to rid myself of that pesky sling. I even tried shooting the Colt with my left hand, though that turned out to not be such a great idea. It made my shoulder hurt like blazes.

I was itching to track down Galt Smathers. I'd worked it through in my mind and prayed on it. I was convinced that he was my bushwhacker. He had motive, means, and inclination. I suspected that he still rode Samuel's horse.

If Smathers thought he'd killed me, he would be unsuspecting prey.

There I sat, back on the gallery, sipping morning coffee. I watched Big Red prancing around the corral. I sure missed being on his back. Of course, he'd earned his keep while I was laid up, as several mares were pregnant. Yes, I was itching to hit the trail.

"Jack chase bad *tabu tosa*?" asked Blue Flower.

Chase the cowardly White man? I nodded and stroked Zeb's mane. He'd healed up quite nicely thanks to Blue Flower's poultices. He, too, had an itch to pursue Smathers.

She knew that it was something I had to do. She was about to speak, when her eyes opened wide. "Baby come!" she announced and headed inside the house.

Buck was passing by.

"Buck! Fetch Kate! The baby's coming!" I called out and followed Blue Flower.

I filled a pot and placed it on the stove to warm water, so I couldn't have been more than a couple of minutes behind. I entered the bedroom with Kate behind me. There lay a smiling but sweating Blue Flower with a newborn baby swathed in her arms. I was amazed. How could this have happened so fast?

"Women on the frontier can't waste time," chided Kate with a smile, as she went to work cleaning Blue Flower and the baby.

I stood dumbfounded.

Blue Flower looked up at me with loving eyes. "Is *wa'ipu onaa*, Jack."

I had a daughter. Now, there'd be four O'Toole children to care for. "What shall we name her?" I asked.

"Jack name," she said.

I shook my head. "Blue Flower name," I insisted.

"Nadua," she responded.

I smiled. "Nadua," I repeated. The name translated to *keeps warm with us*.

Blue Flower gave me a loving look. She hadn't forgotten our conversation before Nadua decided to enter the world. "Jack must hunt." She said it firmly, as though confirming that this was something that a man—a warrior—must do.

"Three days," I responded. I reckoned my shoulder would be up to the task. "What do you think, Zeb?" My wolf companion gave a low bark and nuzzled my hand. He was ready. I looked back at Blue Flower. "I'm going to see if Mukwooru will join me."

Those words apparently reassured Blue Flower, as she quickly nodded agreement.

———

THE NEXT COUPLE of days were a whirlwind of pulling together supplies mixed with helping Blue Flower with our boys whenever I could.

One of Collins's hands had dropped by a newspaper, and we sat at the kitchen table pouring over its contents. It was late summer, and a presidential election loomed ahead. There were plenty of threats written about how the states would secede if Abraham Lincoln was elected. I reckoned that Stephen Douglas and John Breckinridge would effectively cancel each other out by spreading the Democrat Party vote between them. John Bell didn't have a prayer of winning far as I could figure. When and if any serious violence happened, I was committed to being here at Rising Cross Ranch. This meant that I must be efficient in my hunt of Galt Smathers.

In my brief experience on this earth of dealing with evil hombres, the likes of Smathers, I found that they were like snakes in that they didn't stray far from their nest. My first task would be to locate the viper's nest.

How might I deal with Smathers, when I found him? That was a huge question. He certainly deserved to die. It wouldn't do to take him back to Sheriff Maier. I got to thinking on what my pa had taught me from the Good Book. I believe it was the Book of Deuteronomy that advised something like when God delivers the enemy, you strike him down and totally destroy him. You make no bargain with him or show mercy. That was pretty harsh. Sadly, the same could be applied to the White man's conquest of the Indians. For now, I had to place the fate of my Indian brothers behind me and focus on Smathers. No mercy, indeed.

FOUR
SURPRISE

I RODE easy-like into the Comanche encampment. An early morning mist gave the village a surreal feel. There were a couple of the *numunuu* who recognized me riding tall on Big Red's saddle. I wore buckskins and carried my bow and arrow along with Bowie knife, my trusty Colt revolver, and the Sharps carbine. I had a packhorse in tow, but it was loaded with more gifts for Spirit Talker and Buffalo Hump than it was with supplies for my hunt.

I rode up to Spirit Talker's teepee. "Mukwooru!" I called.

Prairie Flower peeked from the teepee flap, saw me, and smiled. "He come," she said, motioning him to come. I saw enough of her to note that she was with child.

Spirit Talker emerged with a broad smile. "Welcome Pohya Isa. *Ana o'a hi'it.*"

I dismounted a embraced my brother. "*Ana o'a hi'it.*" I echoed, always up for Comanche cooking. Zeb trotted over and nuzzled Spirit Talker. Our reunion was complete.

Spirit Talker invited me to a seat beside the fire while Prairie Flower cooked. "What bring Pohya Isa to Penateka Comanche?" he asked.

I pulled back the left shoulder of my buckskin shirt to reveal the terrible scar left by Smathers's bullet. "*Hoikwa*," I replied.

My Comanche brother perked up at the suggestion of a hunt. "*Tosa* shoot Pohya Isa?"

Diverting her eyes from my wound, Prairie Flower interrupted with our meal of elk steak garnished with wild vegetables and berries. It looked absolutely delicious. "How Blue Flower?" she asked.

"We have *onaa*. She is named Nadua," I responded with a grin.

"*Taa Narumi* pleased," she stated. She had adopted our habit of mixing English and Comanche.

"Indeed. God is pleased." Interjected Spirit Talker. He nodded toward Prairie Flower. "We soon add to *numunuu*." He chewed thoughtfully on a strip of elk steak. "Tell me more of this hunt."

"A man named Galt Smathers tortured and hung friends of mine and stole a horse I had gifted to one. The law would not arrest him. I believe he bushwhacked me and nearly killed Zeb." I ruffled back the fur on Zeb's side, revealing the long scar left by Smathers's knife. "Will you hunt with me?"

Spirit Talker and Prairie Flower exchanged glances. I caught her nod of approval in my peripheral vision. "*Hoikwa*," he said enthusiastically. It was clear that he relished the opportunity to hunt human prey. He smiled and ran his finger in a cutting motion across his forehead.

I laughed. "No scalps."

With the meal finished, I motioned Spirit Talker to go

outside. I led him to my packhorse and began untying the load. "I have brought gifts from Blue Flower and me." I hefted a large bundle, carried it to the teepee entrance, and opened it to display a veritable cornucopia of goods.

Prairie Flower heard the bustle outside and stepped from the teepee, almost tripping over the horde of jewelry, clothing, a cooking pot, a Bowie knife, and more. She dropped to her knees and laughed giddily with delight.

It was infectious, as Spirit Talker and I joined in her joy.

"How is Buffalo Hump?" I inquired.

"*Ap* not well. Grow old." Spirit Talker lamented his father's aging.

The notorious war chief of the Penateka Comanche had enjoyed many moons on the lands of his forefathers. He had been so fearsome a warrior that it seemed almost unjust that he would likely die peacefully and not in battle. He surely reveled in his son being a strong leader and tribal shaman and his daughter marrying a good *tosa* —namely me.

"Buffalo Hump talk in sleep of battle to sea," added Spirit Talker, shaking his head. Buffalo Hump had led roughly a thousand Comanche warriors back in 1840 on what was called by Whites *The Great Raid* through Central Texas nearly to the gulf waters, burning Linnville to the ground and damaging Victoria. He famously brought his *numunuu* home with few casualties. He later regretted the missed opportunity to engage Texas Ranger Captain Rip Ford at the Battle of Little Robe Creek nearly two decades later.

"Buffalo Hump proud of Mukwooru," I stated.

"*Hoikwa* in morning," retorted Spirit Talker.

WE DEPARTED from the village just as the sun peeked over the eastern horizon. I had enjoyed a brief meeting with Buffalo Hump the night before. He was indeed aging, and it showed in his bearing and speech. He was but a shadow of the warrior he'd been. Later, I explained to Spirit Talker all that I knew of Smathers from his appearance to his horse and what I observed of his habits. It wasn't so difficult to describe the very embodiment of evil.

As we rode out, I could tell that Spirit Talker had something heavy weighing on his mind.

"What's bothering you?" I asked.

"*Peeka* Smathers?" he asked.

I sighed. "If we must."

Spirit Talker was well aware of my habit of doling out mercy whenever possible. From what I'd described of Smathers and the fact that he'd already attempted to kill me, he was seeking assurance as to my intentions. Capture or death would contribute to our tactics in stalking the killer.

With the ongoing encroachment of White settlers, the Penateka Comanche had moved their encampment far up toward the headwaters of the Pedernales River. It was safer and game was still plentiful.

We decided to give Fredericksburg a wide berth, given the increased predations of Kiowa and some Comanche. There was no point in riling the locals. Besides, they were already overwrought as to the fears swirling about over slavery. Most settlers around the town were of German heritage and deeply appreciative of the opportunities afforded them by emigrating to America. My conversation with Will McGregor during my recent visit included passing along the community talk of secession and how it was deeply concerning. It seemed that big trouble was forecast if Lincoln won in November.

"Where *tosa* be?" mused Spirit Talker with his enigmatic smile. He rubbed his hands together at the prospect of finding Smathers's trail and hunting him down.

"*Tosa* likely feeling good," I replied. "Figure he thinks he killed me." Experience had already taught me that men like Smathers tended to gloat over their evil deeds. That led to overconfidence and inevitable carelessness. "Bet he's still hanging around Fredericksburg."

It was like old times, just me and Spirit Talker hunting together. Of course, the times really weren't all that old. It'd been five years since I'd saved him from the mountain lion attack, an event that began a close friendship.

My plan was to reach Fredericksburg after dark. I reckoned to seek out McGregor and have him put us up for the night. He also would probably know whether Smathers was in or around the town. Here were places a man of Smathers's dark inclinations could hide and even turn a dollar or two from his lawbreaking. Desperadoes like him somehow managed to survive.

We reached the outskirts of before sundown so found a shady spot alongside a creek that fed the Pedernales River to await nightfall. We let the horses drink their fill and graze on the lush grasses close by. Zeb curled up between us, as we sat and took in the beauty of the scene. Cypress and live oak leaves waved in the breeze. Its very peacefulness was rather contradictory to our purposes. However, this very peace afforded us the strength of spirit necessary to employ the skills needed to bring Smathers to justice. Justice? One way or another, justice would be served.

"What Pohya Isa do if big fight?" asked Spirit Talker.

It took me a moment to realize that he was referring to the nation and not our hunt. "My *numunuu* would be in danger. We may have to leave Texas." I was thinking that the threats we'd endured as abolitionists would increase if the slave states seceded from the Union. "I believe men will be called to fight. That will leave many places without defense."

Spirit Talker nodded. "Comanche fight Comanche, too."

I was well aware of the on-again-off-again relationships among the thirteen Comanche subtribes. A small slight could set Quahadi against Nokonis or Penateka against Tenawa. When they weren't warring against each other, they'd be squabbling with Kiowas or Utes or Apache. The White man was the enemy-in-common of most of the Indian nations. Regardless of race or culture, these conflicts seemed to be part of the fundamental nature of humans. I'd heard that Mexico, the neighboring nation south of Texas, was constantly embroiled with internal rebellions. Many Texans feared an uprising of slaves, though any organized slave rebellion seemed highly unlikely. Nevertheless, conflict or its likelihood seemed to abound. I took a long, pondering look at the distant hills. "They sure can come up with reasons to fight. Doesn't seem to take much. George sent us a letter. He heard that someone had found a thick black substance oozing from the ground. They call it oil, and it's apparently valuable as a lubricant, salve, and fuel. He believes men will pursue it like they seek gold."

"There be big battle. Many *kooitu*," suggested Spirit Talker. "*Numunuu* with much hate. *Tosa* no think."

I had to agree. Folks whose minds are driven by hateful passions mostly don't think straight. The plantation owners whose livelihoods depended on slaves fed those hatreds, stoked passions, and employed the political sway that could plunge the nation into a war against itself. Men I'd dealt with, like Galt Smathers, Rolf Schultz, and Burt Colthwaite, were like a vanguard of the evil that might yet befall the nation. Spirit Talker's probing question as to what I might do to protect my family while standing firm for my principles, weighed heavily. "I expect we're going to have to be ready if and when the time comes." I wondered, too, where Sam Houston stood about all of this. As governor, he had surely found himself in a dilemma over slavery. His wife Margaret had long ago broken him of drinking alcohol, and he had been baptized into the Baptist Church by immersion in Little Rocky Creek near Independence, Texas. I reckoned he had to be a man of strong Christian ethic, yet he faced strong political pressure. Being realistic and despite my wishes to the contrary, I expected he would wind up yielding to the pro-slavery forces. That would leave the question of whether Texas would join in any national conflict? "Yep. We just might have to leave Rising Cross—at least, for a time."

Spirit Talker nodded agreement and looked off at the sun sinking on the western horizon. "We go now," he said with an arm motion toward Fredericksburg.

I reckoned it would be smart to avoid the main street, given the anti-Indian sentiment of the town. With my buckskins and bow and arrows, the folks might mistake me for a Redman. Zeb seemed to sense that our quarry was near at hand, as his ears were up, and he kept sniffing the air. We cautiously made our way along a narrow path that eventually brought us behind McGregor's shop. We dismounted and led our horses through the back door of the stable. "Will!" I called out in a low voice.

"Who goes?" came the response, along with the tell-tale sound of a rifle hammer being pulled back.

"It's me...Jack and Spirit Talker," I replied.

McGregor's eyes grew wide, and his jaw nearly dropped to his boot tops. "B-b-but yer dead," he declared.

I stepped into the light cast by the forge.

"It's a miracle!" announced McGregor. He glanced about furtively. "Stay back. The sheriff's comin' in a minute to fetch his horse."

The last thing I sought was to reengage with Sheriff Maier. We backtracked and hitched our mounts behind the stable, hanging low in the shadows of the night. We could hear the sheriff thanking McGregor for replacing a couple of horseshoes. After a brief conversation, the sheriff departed, and the coast was clear.

McGregor stuck his head out the rear door and motioned us inside. "Lord almighty, Jack. There's a fellow in town claiming he rid the world of you. Blew you from the saddle an' left yuh fer dead. Stella and I ne'er figured to see yuh again."

"You must mean Galt Smathers. He nearly succeeded, my friend. Bushwhacked me on the Pinta Trail, but the Lord was with me." I pulled back enough of my buckskin shirt to reveal the ugly scare from Smathers's bullet.

McGregor shook his head. "Told yuh he be an evil sort, Jack." He glanced over at Spirit Talker. "Good to see you, Mukwooru."

Spirit Talker smiled, as he was impressed that McGregor had recalled his Comanche name.

Undeterred, I continued my account of the bushwhacking. "Smathers is a coward. He nearly killed Zeb, too, but I think he took a bite out of him. He gave Zeb a nasty wound with his knife."

"Might account for the bandana he be wearin' 'round his neck," McGregor noted.

"I don't want to deal with the man here in Fredericksburg. The sheriff's not likely to be any help, and I don't want innocent folks getting hurt." I rubbed my cold hands at the smithy forge, as the evening had introduced a late summer chill.

"Yuh might be in luck. Folks in town tain't comfortable. Been pressin' the sheriff to kick him out. Praise the Lord, Sheriff told me Smathers be talkin' 'bout leavin' town."

"Not much *hoikwa*," observed Spirit Talker with a disappointed expression. Well, yuh can stay here tonight.

I smiled at my Comanche brother. He was right that this hunt was turning out to be far too easy. "We'll give him a head start," I said with a wink. I turned to McGregor. "We need to hurry his leaving Fredericksburg."

"He owes me for fixin' his tack. If I press him fer payment, he may leave sooner," said McGregor.

"I don't want you placing yourself in danger, my friend."

Just then, Stella appeared. "Why look who's here and back from the dead! Y'all must be hungry," she chided, then smiled at her husband. "What are you dallying for, Will? Let's eat."

We needed no arm-twisting, as we dutifully filed along behind her and into their modest cabin. There was ample space around the table, and the McGregors were always pleased to share what bounty they could offer. This evening, we were treated to a rarity: pronghorn. The critters were very difficult to hunt owing to the great difficulty in getting close enough to shoot the flighty animals.

"What was heaven like, Jack?" asked Stella, sort of tongue in cheek.

"Didn't quite get there," I said with a laugh.

Stella turned serious. "What are you figuring to do after you bring this Smathers fellow to justice?" she asked.

"Reckon God has a plan," I replied almost too reflexively. I suppose it was what might be called a pat answer when a person—especially a Christian—was uncertain of the future.

She gave me *the look*.

McGregor shrugged, and Spirit Talker smirked, given that he'd asked me a similar question.

I sighed. "It's complicated," I said, stating the obvious. "Y'all know I'm not one to run from trouble. If our nation turns to war between states, my days of spiriting away escaped slaves on cattle drives must likely end. Do I stay at Rising Cross Ranch? Will my family be safe? Do I dare try to influence political decisions in Austin? Do I become a martyr over slavery? Or, should I take my family north and hide away at our friend George Freeman's ranch up near Fort Laramie?"

"Much danger in Texas," noted Spirit Talker.

McGregor nodded. "Aye, Jack could sign his death warrant. Even we be in danger," he said with conviction.

I took a sip of coffee to buy time to gather my thoughts. "The newspapers are filled with support for slavery. Abolitionists are condemned, and folks use that as an excuse to wreak havoc upon us. I feel called to influence the course of history, but haven't been able to carry much impact. Helping a mere handful of slaves to escape seems trifling compared to the scope of the problem. Oh, it was important to those we saved, but a mere speck on the landscape of the huge issues we face."

Spirit Talker stared at me. "Jack miss trail sign."

I gave him a questioning look.

"What you call newspaper is answer." He rolled his eyes at what he felt was all-too-obvious.

My expression was unchanged.

"Jack tell story to newspapers," Spirit Talker added with exasperation.

His wisdom finally hit me like a mule's kick. I could take my family away from immediate danger and share with the newspapers my story of fighting against slavery. The northern press would suck it up like a herd of thirsty longhorns. If I could inspire peace, spread light in the darkness, all the better. It would vastly expand the reach of my anti-slavery message. "That's a great idea, my brother."

"Jack strong *sunipu*," stated Spirit Talker

Indeed, my medicine was strong as bulwarked by my faith in God.

Smiles surrounded the table. We'd sleep well this night.

———————

NEXT MORNING, I awakened to the clanging of smithy tools on red-hot steel. If there was anything that might wake the dead, it'd have to be a smithy's hammer on steel. I yawned, stretched, slipped on my moccasins, and stood shaking the straw from myself. I felt Big Red's eyes laughing at me as I picked the last pieces of hay from the fringe on my shirt. I motioned Zeb to give Spirit Talker a nudge and headed to where McGregor was banging away on a branding iron.

"Mornin', Jack," announced McGregor. "I hear tell Smathers is inclined to head eastward today to see what's stirring around Austin."

It was more like the man felt drawn to trouble—finding it or making it.

"Reggie tells me that Smathers bought extra supplies, including plenty of ammunition. He'll be picking up his tack from me this morning." McGregor motioned me toward the cabin and went back to his hammering.

Approaching the cabin door, I could smell bacon cooking on the skillet. I paused to enjoy the aroma, and Spirit Talker and Zeb nearly bumped into me.

Stella served up a delicious breakfast. It wasn't long before Spirit Talker and I found ourselves standing at the front window of McGregor's cabin and sipping coffee. My attention was drawn to a dark-clad figure leading a black horse by a tether. It was Smathers coming to pick up his tack from McGregor. He still had the temerity to possess the horse he'd stolen from Samuel. I felt my blood boil up just a tad at the sight of it.

Spirit Talker nudged me. "Easy prey, but much danger," he observed.

Smathers led his horse to the smithy shop. As he began to pay McGregor for repairing his tack, he caught sight of Big Red in the stable.

"Son of a…" and he grabbed McGregor's hammer and struck the side of his head.

McGregor lifted an arm to slightly deflect the blow, likely saving his life. But, he lay knocked out cold.

Smathers grabbed his carbine and turned to the cabin.

I was still looking out the window and beginning to get excited about the prospect of hunting Smathers. "Looks like he'll be leaving. We'll let him get a couple of hours ahead of us. He'll be easy to track, but we don't want to get ourselves killed when we catch up to him." I took a long sip of coffee. "We're much obliged for that great breakfast, Stella," I said with a turn from the window. My jaw dropped.

"Not so easy to foller me O'Toole," growled the voice behind the gaping muzzle of a Sharps carbine. Stella lay out cold, crumpled at Smathers's feet with blood oozing from a gash along the side of her head. He'd likely already disposed of my smithy friend. I was well aware of what a slug from a Sharps could do to a human body. One delivered by Smathers had nearly cost me my shoulder.

I stood helpless and empty-handed before this destroyer of life, this very epitome of evil.

"I reckon to finish yuh, O'Toole." Smathers's words spewed vile hatred in every syllable.

I feared that the devil was calling, he knew my name.

"That there wolf move a muscle, an' I'll kill yuh, the Injun, an' the woman afore he gits me." The sheer vileness bled from every pore of the creature's being. But for the immediacy of the moment, I might have been drawn to my pa's teaching me about evil in the book of Romans, how men's throats are open graves, their tongues practice deceit, and the poison of vipers is on their lips. Surely, that described the very essence of Smathers.

Time seemed to stand still.

Spirit Talker was mostly hidden by my body. I could feel his hand remove the Bowie knife from its sheath behind my back.

Smathers's toothless grin turned into a broad, dark smile that reeked of the devil himself. The empty blackness of his eyes would put a rattlesnake's glare to shame. He raised the muzzle of the carbine, aiming it at my head. He never saw the flash of the blade, as Spirit Talker threw it at full force. Zeb leaped. The knife plowed deep into Smathers's shoulder. The muzzle of the Sharps exploded in flame, but the force of the knife striking flesh and bone destroyed any accuracy as the bullet went above my head.

Zeb's jaws were at the outlaw's throat, tearing at the protective bandana. I charged headlong into Smathers, driving him to the ground while pushing Zeb away. I yanked the Bowie knife from the outlaw's shoulder. It had delivered a terrible—a mortal—cut, as blood gushed forth. I sat atop Smathers with his arms pinned beneath my knees and stared into his vacant, soulless eyes. In this moment of my glaring angrily into the murderer's pain-contorted face, I could understand why the Comanche and other tribes tortured their victims. They surely wanted to release all the pent-up fear and hate they felt toward the people who brought disease and death upon them. I felt no call by God to show mercy. Smathers was a dying man, and nothing would save him from that fate. I sat there upon him, awaiting his end. He muttered something that sounded vile as blood dribbled from his gaping, gasping lips. Seconds later, he emitted his final breath, a wheezy, bloody exhalation. His black eyes stared vacantly into whatever void his death occupied. I pulled his eyelids shut.

I felt no joy, no satisfaction. I was almost sorry that I hadn't personally delivered the knife that ended the life of this disgusting excuse for manhood. It was as though Spirit Talker had robbed me of avenging Sheesha's and Samuel's deaths. Then again, he'd saved my life—all of our lives. I felt Zeb's warm breath beside me and placed an arm around his shoulders. He'd been robbed of the kill as well.

As I got up, Spirit Talker did what I considered terribly uncivilized, terribly ungodly. He strode purposely over, bent down, and sliced away Galt Smathers's scalp. "No *tumah tuyai,*" he passionately declared. In Spirit Talker's Comanche world, there'd be no afterlife for this sorry excuse for a human. Realizing what he'd done in the passion of the moment, he dropped the scalp like a hot potato. "God forgive Mukwooru," he begged. In a way, he had satisfied both his Comanche spirit and God.

I stood facing my Comanche brother with my hands on his shoulders. "You need not worry my friend. God understands." His quickness and skill with the knife had surely saved our lives. Thinking back to when I'd saved him from the mountain lion and the many times we'd saved each other's lives, there would be no life debt— just our eternal brotherhood.

A groggy McGregor staggered into the cabin and scanned the room. Seeing Stella, he wobbled over and kneeled at her side. She was just beginning to come around.

"So sorry to bring this trouble on you, Will," I said by way of heartfelt apology.

"He woulda kilt us all, Jack."

"Guess we'd better let Sheriff Maier know. Bad as Smathers was, we'd better not tell him that Mukwooru killed him. They'd figure it to be Indian savagery and want his hide. When he asks, I'll take credit."

Spirit Talker nodded agreement. He was all too aware of the White man's prejudices. "Hunt over," he said. "We go home."

———

I TOOK it upon myself to fetch Sheriff Maier. There was nothing to hide, and I reckoned he'd be quite relieved to have had concerns about Smathers ended.

Maier's white face turned paler as he entered the cabin and surveyed the scene. I feared he might throw up. "Oh my." He gestured. "Tell me again what happened."

I explained the sequence of events once again and pointed to where the slug from Smathers's Sharps carbine had embedded itself in the wall above where I'd been standing.

"How'd he lose his hair?" asked Smathers.

"Wolf tore into him," I replied.

"Hmmm," mused the sheriff. "Looks like a knife cut to me," he said with a glance at Spirit Talker.

"You seen what a wolf's teeth can do, sheriff. They can slice like scissors." I gestured toward my canine companion. "Besides, Smathers was already dead, when Zeb here got to him."

Maier seemed sufficiently satisfied with my explanation. He turned to me. "What about that hoss you said he stole?"

"Happy to take him home, sheriff," I offered. "He does wear my brand."

"And burial?"

"I'll handle that," offered a still slightly groggy McGregor.

"That's fine by me. I can say the folks here in Fredericksburg will be plumb relieved to be done of this here rattlesnake." The sheriff expressed his heartfelt relief and bid us a *good-day*.

By now, Stella was sitting in a chair with her wound having been gently tended to with one of Spirit Talker's healing poultices. "Bless you Jack and Mukwooru for saving our lives," she said.

The memory of facing death, seeing the knife fly, hearing the explosion from the carbine, and felling Smathers was becoming less of a blur. It had all happened with blazing speed. God's final justice had been wrought.

FIVE

TROUBLE THIS WAY COMES

WE DECIDED it was best not to hang around Fredericksburg and left it to McGregor to deal with the distasteful duty of disposing of Galt Smathers's body. I wondered if there was a grave deep enough to fully contain his evilness.

We could have gone directly to Spirit Talker's village, but decided to first visit the spot where I'd buried Sheesha and Samuel. It seemed to be the right thing to do, even though it took us considerably out of our way. Zeb trotted along with us. He served as extra security.

By now, we had become extra cautious, as passions throughout Texas were getting out of hand. We decided to make camp at the intersection of the Pinta Trail and Pedernales River. Once we reached the burial spot, we reckoned to head northwest over the rough hills to Spirit Talker's village.

The river barely lived up to that moniker, as the dry summer had taken its toll. Nevertheless, there was water enough in pools to meet the needs of us and our horses. We built a small cooking fire and roasted some smoked elk steaks McGregor had provided to us. They didn't exactly make for a mouth-watering meal, but they'd been well-seasoned and hit the spot after having ridden a few hours on the trail. Washed down with such coffee as we were able to brew, we'd not go hungry.

"*Tosa peeka* plenty," blurted Spirit Talker in our accustomed Comanche-English mix.

I nodded. "If there's war, *tosa* will leave homesteads to fight. Comanche, Kiowa, Ute, and others will kill settlers. Plenty *peeka*." I was being honest with myself. Feelings were running ever-stronger in Texas in support of slavery, and I reckoned this was happening throughout the southern states. It didn't take much mental noodling to realize that things could get out of hand in a hurry. No one—not even Sam Houston—could stem the tide of war once it gained full momentum.

"Pohya Isa *sunipu* not enough," observed Spirit Talker.

He was right. Walks With Wolves didn't possess strong enough medicine to change the course of the inevitable. I could only hope that I could reach folks by writing to newspapers and praying that they'd publish my messages as based in my faith-based cries to end slavery. Meanwhile, I needed to figure a safe place to keep my family. However, I'd come to realize that passions were being driven by more than the issue of slavery. What, after all, would make someone that owned no slaves want to fight to preserve that institution? I had read a news article a few weeks back that described a condition the writer called popular sovereignty whereby the leaders of a state and its government are created and sustained by the consent of its people, who, in turn, are the source of all political legitimacy. It was the basic principle upon which the United States had been founded. Folks voluntarily gave up some of their natural freedom so as to secure protection from the dangers inherent in the freedom of others inclined to evil deeds. I reckoned that even an unschooled person, illiterate if you will, might be persuaded to fight to defend the preservation of a peaceful existence. As God says in the Bible, loving your neighbor as yourself is the second great commandment. Would preserving the right to sovereignty be enough to die for? Were their powerful forces that could create the perception that with the abolition of slavery, such sovereignty would be lost and thus cause men to want to lay down their lives. "Darkness looms," I stated unequivocally.

"Pohya Isa live with Mukwooru?" suggested Spirit Talker.

"That could bring danger to you," I responded.

Spirit Talker poked thoughtfully at the fire with a stick.

"I'm thinking we might head farther west, beyond *tosa* reach," I suggested. Maybe I was fooling myself, as Whites seemed to be everywhere. There was no total escape from them, plus I also had to be concerned with hostile Indians. While the Penateka Comanche were my friends, their enemies were my enemies.

"Live in mountains," urged Spirit Talker. "Maybe George?"

I laughed. "Bad winter," I observed. Cold weather didn't suit me. Our friend George Freeman's ranch was a great place to visit anytime but winter, so far as I was concerned. "There are hidden places west of Palo Duro Canyon where we could live well and be safe."

"Utes and Quahadi no like," observed Spirit Talker. "Cheyenne make trouble, too."

"Might be better than Whites," I said with an ironic tone.

"This Lincoln you say cause war?" queried Spirit Talker.

"There are what they call political parties, people of like minds as to the future of the nation. The party they call Democrat is split in two. The other party—the one of Abraham Lincoln—will surely win. It will ignite the fire of war. Those that want to keep the nation together will fight to keep those that try to leave." It was an awkward way to explain to my Comanche brother who had been brought up for most of his life in the culture of the Indian. Land wasn't owned, manhood was proven on hunts or in battle, women had a voice up to a point, and they lived lives etched over many centuries.

"Mukwooru try to understand," said a confused Spirit Talker, shaking his head resignedly. "Can God stop?"

"I think God will let men sort it out. He gave us free will, the freedom to choose our destiny, our future."

Spirit Talker nodded. "Pohya Isa choose to keep family safe," he stated flatly.

"I must consider more than myself. That would be selfish."

"Selfish?" he asked.

"Yes. Do what I want without thinking of others."

"Selfish not good," he observed.

"God wishes us to be selfless, to consider others in what we do." I found myself preaching a bit.

Spirit Talker yawned.

I would take first watch.

————

WE AWAKENED to an uncharacteristically misty morning. Maybe the gloom was appropriate to our honoring the graves of Sheesha and Samuel.

We broke camp and headed south. In the two hours it took to reach the gravesite, we encountered nary a soul. In fact, it was eerily quiet save for the occasional chirping of birds. I had scratched my initials into a rock to mark the place alongside the trail where we'd buried the couple, so the site was easy to find.

We finally reached the spot, dismounted, and led our horses off the trail into the woods about fifty feet to where the graves were located. I looked around. It had not been that long ago, but there was no trace of the cross that marked the graves. In fact, the soil at the gravesite was depressed. Someone or something had been digging around and done a terrible job of disguising their deed. What had happened?

Zeb growled, sensing that something wasn't right. Perhaps, he recalled Galt Smathers.

I scanned the woods to be certain all was safe, then stepped close to the graves while Spirit Talker kept watch. I stood for a moment, then grabbed my shovel and dug around. "Oh my!" I blurted. The bodies were missing! Who or what could have done this? There was no sign of animals destroying the graves. No, this had been done by human animals.

Spirit Talker led his pony away. "Bad *sunipu*," he said from the safety of the trail. The sacred nature of the buried dead had been violated. It was one of the few times that I saw fear in his eyes. I understood. Even his faith in God was not yet sufficient to overcome his ingrained cultural ways.

"Somebody stole the bodies!" I declared. "Who would have done such a thing? How would they have known to look here? What would drive anyone to desecrate the site."

"Come. We go," insisted Spirit Talker.

I was at a loss. Scanning the area, there were no obvious clues. I refilled the empty graves and stuck the partially destroyed cross back in the ground. This place would at least be a memorial. Wasn't long before Spirit Talker and I departed the trail and began to head due west.

We traveled barely a mile before coming upon a clearing featuring an almost-dry creek. Out on the frontier, a person never enters an open area without first scanning the area to assure that its safe to expose oneself. We looked about, nodded to each other, and proceeded forward. The open space was easily a couple of hundred yards wide and flat as a pancake. We'd gone about halfway, when we came upon a blackened area where there'd been a sizable bonfire.

"Why would anyone be setting a blaze like this?" I ventured to Spirit Talker.

We both dismounted to inspect the spot. A few burned logs remained. The why of such a fire kept rumbling around in my head. There were no signs of any large party having camped close by that might account for such a large fire.

"Pohya Isa! Here!" said Spirit Talker, pointing animatedly.

Bones! There were human bones strewn about among some of the burned logs. I couldn't be certain, but they very well could have been those of Sheesha and Samuel. My mind recoiled at my realization of what must have happened. Galt Smathers! After he figured he'd killed me, he determined to get rid of any evidence of the bodies. Of course, he'd been sloppy in not hiding the gravesite, but it'd likely been enough for him to have dealt with the disposal of the moldering bodies. What an utterly evil man!

"*Tosa tabu!*" intoned Spirit Talker. Indeed, Smathers was a craven coward.

While Smathers had met his fate at the end of Spirit Talker's knife, it did raise the specter of who accompanied him when Sheesha and Samuel had been murdered. There'd been enough hoofprints to suggest as many as four shod horses had witnessed the scene. Smathers stole Samuel's horse, the only horse with a sufficiently distinct hoofprint and gait to enable us to both track and identify him. Others had escaped and likely would never be found. I could only hope the deed weighed heavily on their consciousnesses.

I looked around. The silence roared in my ears.

My thoughts turned to Blue Flower and our children. Would escaping the threats posed by the possibility of war be the right course? Where might my influence be best applied? God was with me. I sensed that much potential lay ahead.

We rode mindlessly westward, stopping occasionally to rest the horses, watering them when the opportunity arose. A wooded glade lay ahead, and we decided to camp for the night. The emotions of the day had taken more from us than we'd realized.

"Why Pohya Isa fight?" asked Spirit Talker, as he built a small fire to cook as well as take the chill away.

It might have been easy to have spouted out something along the lines of God telling me to, but there was more to it. It was more about putting my faith into practice. I added some kindling to the fire. "I fight because I care. Many don't or are on an ungodly path. I think a life of faith in God life takes us on paths that help us grow. Great growth requires daring to be part of something bigger than self, something that may involve risk of my own life." I'd said a mouthful and hoped that

Spirit Talker's grasp of English was enough to understand.

Spirit Talker looked up at me. The light from the fire flickered across his face. "Jack Pohya Isa. Isa brave, loyal. *Natsuitu pihi*. Isa tough, protect family. Isa leader, speak for all who follow. Strong *sunipu*." He was laying out the characteristics of the wolfpack leader.

I nodded. The leader of the pack was about strength of heart, strong medicine, trust, moral character, and risk for the benefit of all whom he led. Little wonder at my belief that God had sent Zeb to me. My wolf companion served to reinforce the characteristics that God expected from me.

Importantly, Spirit Talker understood. He looked back into the fire. The flames sputtered and flared. He looked up into the vastness of the sky. An eagle soared high above us. "*Kwihnai* no fly in cave."

Indeed, eagles didn't fly in caves. They flew high where they could search for their prey. They were free to do what God created them for. I found myself reaching the conclusion that it wouldn't do to run off and hide from threats while sending out messages to newspapers to inspire those fighting against slavery. It was a risk worth taking. "*Kwihnai*," I murmured. I glanced over at Zeb. "No offense, big guy. *Kwihnai* flies high but is no leader of a pack." I ruffled the big wolf's furry neck and received a slobbery lick in response.

We had just laid down on our bedrolls when Zeb stood abruptly with ears alert and tail unmoving. Our fire had died out, and all was shrouded in darkness. A hazy cover of clouds screened out most of the starlight, and there was only a crescent moon.

Hugging the ground, Spirit Talker and I heeded Zeb's

warning and eased away toward some nearby scrub bushes.

But for the distant bark of a coyote, all lay in silence. Then...then there was the telltale click of a gun being cocked. In the dim light, we could barely see our hands in front of our faces. Everything was in shadows. Our bedrolls were simply dark lumps on the bare earth. A muzzle flashed from perhaps fifty feet away, and an explosion rocked the landscape. A slug ripped through my bedroll. We stayed hidden. Another click and another muzzle flash and explosion, and a bullet ripped through Spirit Talker's bedroll. We heard footsteps running away, then the sound of hoofbeats. They were shod. "Got 'em, Digger." Those were the only words we heard as the attackers fled.

Spirit Talker and I looked at each other in the darkness, as concern spread across our faces. Zeb remained standing. It was as though he sensed that he shouldn't pursue whoever had fired into our camp. In the dark, even a wolf appreciated when the odds were stacked against him. Bushwhackers on the run would have the upper hand. For all we knew, they could have missed on purpose to lure us into a trap.

Danger had come our way. Whoever it was figured they'd dispatched us. Who were they? Who was Digger? Galt Smathers's cronies immediately came to mind. Why had they sought to kill us?

SIX
CO-CONSPIRATORS

WITH THE FIRST light of dawn, we began searching for sign. In their haste to kill us and run, the attackers left plenty of clues. If, in fact, they were associated with Smathers, I did wonder why they would have waited so long? I suspected they may have been distracted with other endeavors.

"*Hoikwa tabu*," ventured Spirit Talker.

I nodded. Yes, we'd hunt the cowards.

We found the tracks of two horses, one with a broken shoe. From footprints left in the damp soil, we determined that one of the attackers was heavy while his companion was much lighter and had smaller feet. There were no other signs, not even spent cartridges. The men escaped northwestward toward Fredericksburg.

"They might visit McGregor to get that shoe replaced," I suggested.

Spirit Talker chuckled. "*Tosa* put metal on horse hooves. Make easy *hoikwa*."

I didn't fully agree but it did generally enable distinguishing between Indian ponies and White men's horses.

Now and then, Indians might ride stolen horses that were shod. That aside, we knew that we were likely dealing with White men, one large and one smaller. From the sound of the shots and the damage done to our bedrolls, I judged that they'd used a powerful rifle. Most likely, they used the *Big Fifty*, a Sharps carbine. "Let's go back to Fredericksburg." I noted that the two attackers' route would intersect the Pinta Trail. We could make better time by taking a more direct route straight for Fredericksburg.

We broke camp and headed out. Mind you, I said a prayer or two. What if Zeb hadn't alerted us?

IT TOOK the better part of the day to reach Fredericksburg. We approached from the south, reaching the Pedernales River. It consisted mostly of pools of brackish standing water, as winter rains and snows loomed ahead. If our attackers rode through the night—an unlikely endeavor—they'd have had a pretty fair head start. As it was, my senses told me that they camped somewhere and would enjoy a leisurely ride here the next day. Reckoning that they'd killed us, their only worries might be bandits or hostile Comanche or Kiowa.

I turned toward Spirit Talker. "Let's check the trail approaching from the east," I said. If my hunch was right and they'd headed for Fredericksburg, we should find their tracks.

We searched, exercising all our skills as experienced hunters but turned up no tracks. Either I'd guessed wrong that they were headed here, or we'd arrived ahead of them. An idea crossed my mind. I gave Spirit Talker a devious look. "*Hoikwa*?" I stated more than asked. The prey would become the hunters.

Spirit Talker returned a broad smile. "*Hoikwa*," he echoed.

If our two attackers were coming here, they'd most likely approach along the south bank of the river. There was plenty of scrub chaparral from which to set an ambush. The sun was hanging well above the horizon, so there was still plenty of light. Then, an idea struck me: bow and arrow!

The hunt was on!

I caught myself. Was what we were about to do strictly vengeance? Was this God's plan? And yet, evil-doers must be punished. If the law wasn't to do it, then who? Were we any better than the vigilantes that tried to lynch me? Well, I reckoned we might be a hair above them, given that they were acting out of rumor and unbridled hatred.

Spirit Talker caught my pause. "*Hoikwa tabu*," he stated firmly. "Is God work!" he added. He pointed to me and himself. "*Tosa tabu*."

He was right. The men had tried to murder us. If not for Zeb's warning, we'd have been in our bedrolls and been killed. I pulled the bow and quiver of arrows from my bedroll. We found a place with high ground on both sides of the trail with cover and a clear view of the approach to Fredericksburg. We'd be close enough to the trail that even an inexperienced bowman couldn't miss. We hobbled our horses out of sight of the trail. Zeb sat beside me, while Spirit Talker found a spot opposite us.

I heard sounds of horses approaching, but the squeaks and squeals of a wagon lurching from rock to rock along the trail hinted that this wasn't our prey. The wagon lumbered by with nary an indication from the driver and passenger that they'd passed by us. I nodded to Spirit Talker and signaled to him that we needed to talk. He gathered his weapons and crossed to my position.

"This could take a long time," I suggested. In reality, I was impatient and—to be perfectly honest—bored. "*Hoikwa.*" I wanted to hunt the two killers.

Spirit Talker understood. We were confident that our prey would travel along this trail along the south bank of the Pedernales. The sun was headed for the horizon. My earlier sense that the killers would camp for the night and arrive in Fredericksburg the next morning sounded more likely. "They camp. We attack at night." I relished the irony of us attacking their campsite just as they'd done to us.

"*Hoikwa* easy," lamented Spirit Talker.

I smiled. "But dangerous." We would be approaching at night with no moon, plus we needed to be certain of our prey. It wouldn't do to kill the wrong men. We set off down the riverside trail with our horses in tow and arrows nocked. A chill wind and dark clouds whipped up as though casting a touch of foreboding on our mission.

We needn't look over our shoulders, as the ever-longer shadows gave evidence of the sun's journey to the horizon. By my estimation, we'd walked about four miles when we caught the distant glow of a campfire. It was a goodly blaze worthy of the killers' overconfidence.

We tethered our mounts to a live oak about fifty feet off the trail. We'd go on foot. Zeb stayed close. His senses were on high alert, so I stroked him to keep him calm. I didn't need him giving us away. What I figured to be a brilliant idea struck me like a log up the side of my head. "Mukwooru," I said while grasping his arm.

Spirit Talker looked curiously at me. We were no more than a hundred yards from our prey.

"*Mukue*," I said as though I'd discovered gold. I scooped up the white dust along the path and began covering myself. By the time I'd tossed an ample amount on myself, I'd become quite ghostly-looking.

Spirit Talker smiled. "*Mukue*," he echoed and began covering himself in white dust.

By the time we were finished, we looked as though we were ghosts emerged from graves in a cemetery. We left a dusty trail as we continued our trek toward the firelight.

At about fifty feet from the campfire, I came upon the men's horses. It took but a moment to confirm that one had a broken shoe. These men were our prey.

I led Spirit Talker out into the center of the trail. "Ahwooooo!" I howled in as ghostlike a voice as I could muster. I repeated it, and Spirit Talker joined in. "Ahwooooo!" went our chorus of ghostly warnings.

The expressions on the two men turned instantly to fear. Eyes widened, and mouths fell open. "Who you be?" shouted one of the men.

"*Peeeeka Tosa!*" said Spirit Talker, sounding like a dead man talking.

"Killers!" I added. "Ahwooooo!"

"Digger, let's git!" hollered one of the men.

"I'm outta here, Tex!"

In the glow of the fire, we likely looked about as ghostly as it was possible to achieve. I could see that both men had wet their pants.

The men suddenly froze with the realization that escape was impossible. We stood between them and their horses. "Nooo, go away! Be gone!" they hollered, panic written large across their faces.

Zeb appeared.

The appearance of a large wolf was too much for the two. They turned with hopes of running.

"Legs," I whispered to Spirit Talker. We each launched arrows that crippled the two.

Now groveling on their knees in excruciating pain and with a wolf's fangs drawing ever nearer, the two were sweating bullets in the chill night air.

"You no good cowards," I said as we stood no more than a dozen feet from the two.

The realization that we weren't spirits simultaneously swept over the two. "Why! You be!" they gasped.

"We're your worst nightmare," I assured them.

Digger and Tex were trapped.

"B-b-but yer dead!" exclaimed Digger.

The arrows protruding from their legs were an angry testament to their cowardly nature.

"We surrender. D-d-don't be shootin' us agin!" pleaded Tex.

We already had arrows nocked and aimed at the men's chests. "You want scalps?" I chided with a glance at Spirit Talker.

Spirit Talker shook his head. "No take *tabu* hair." No self-respecting Comanche wanted the scalps of cowards.

"These *tosa peeka* Sheesha and Samuel."

"Whatcha sayin'?" whimpered Digger.

"Y'all admit to being with Galt Smathers when he killed the two Blacks on the Pinta Trail?"

"We din't wanna do it," pleaded Tex. "My leg's killin' me," he groaned.

"Did you use *isa wasu*?" I asked Spirit Talker.

"What be *isa wasu*?" begged Digger.

"Oh, that would be a poisoned arrow."

The expressions that swept the two men's faces were worth my entertaining the threat of poisoned arrows.

Spirit Talker shook his head, much to the relief of the two murderers.

Zeb growled. He yearned to take a bite or two from these evildoer's hides.

"You are lucky," I assured the two.

"Lucky? How yuh be sayin' thet?" groaned Tex.

"We're going to turn y'all in to Sheriff Maier in Fredericksburg."

Digger's and Tex's bodies sagged with pained relief.

"Easy Zeb," I gently held my wolf companion back. "We're going to take those arrows from your legs. Cause any trouble, and I'll let Zeb tear you apart."

The two nodded vigorously.

What followed was decidedly unpleasant. I gave Spirit Talker the honor of cutting the arrows from the killers' legs. I daresay that he enjoyed the task, as I perversely enjoyed watching. Once the arrows were freed, the wounds were cauterized using the glowing tip of a branch from the campfire. Tex held up fairly well, but Digger passed out.

Once the surgeries were completed, we bound the men securely to nearby live oak trunks. Come morning, we'd take them to Sheriff Maier. Meanwhile, they'd spend a chilly night with plenty of time to reflect on their misdeeds.

I felt a sense of having delivered a Godly brand of justice. I had taken the law into my hands to an extent, but had refrained from the sort of justice delivered by vigilantes. I was determined to do my civic duty and deliver the killers to the law to stand trial for their crimes.

GETTING Digger and Tex into their saddles wasn't easy. Their wounded legs had stiffened overnight, so they endured considerable pain as we tied them into their saddles. We bound their hands behind them. There would be no escaping.

Spirit Talker and I washed away our coating of spirit dust. The ruse had worked spectacularly well and would make for great retelling back home. Mounting up, I led the way toward Fredericksburg with Digger's and Rex's horses on tethers and Spirit Talker bringing up our rear.

About this time and brought on by the methodical plodding of Big Red, my thoughts turned to home. I missed Blue Flower. She was what any self-respecting frontier cowboy could ever dream of, and for me, more. She never complained of my absences but supported and encouraged me. She knew I'd do whatever it took to protect her. Blue Flower was like a mate for my soul. I sensed that we would face ever greater tests, yet had more to give each other and the world. We'd certainly faced dangers, apart and together, and endured. I earnestly believed that God yet had a greater purpose for us. Importantly, I was out here on the frontier, being whoever God gave me the choice to be, not the me chosen by others. God provided endless choices, and thus far, I'd managed to pretty much make the good ones, the ones from my heart.

Fredericksburg came into view. Digger and Tex were sagging in their saddles but would perk up once we reached Sheriff Maier's office and faced the prospect of judge and jury and likely execution. They lacked the glib tongue that had enabled Garth Smathers to worm his way from justice.

———

SHERIFF ED MAIER knew better than to doubt my word. He'd done poorly by me with Garth Smathers and was embarrassed by his inactions that ended with Smathers's death.

We reined in at the jail and untied Digger and Tex from their saddles. We pulled them down none-too-gently. The cauterization had staunched any bleeding from their arrow wounds, not that it mattered given the likelihood of swift justice. Spirit Talker and I pushed them up the steps and through the front door. We didn't bother to knock.

"What!" exclaimed a startled sheriff.

"We have two guests for you, Sheriff Maier."

Maier rolled his eyes, but quickly thought better of it. He'd failed to believe us about Smathers, and that had cost his reputation dearly. "What'd they do, Mr. O'Toole?"

"Murder and attempted murder," I stated matter-of-factly.

Maier turned to Digger and Tex. "This true?" he asked.

The two men half shrugged and half nodded.

"Is this *true*?" Maier asked emphatically.

Zeb sat guardedly beside me and let out a low growl that Digger and Tex surely heard.

"The two Blacks don't count none, an' we missed killin' these two. Injun don't count none either," insisted Digger.

I was ready to lay into them, but held my tongue and my anger.

"These two rode with Garth Smathers, Sheriff. They helped Smathers waylay and kill two free Blacks, Sheesha and Samuel, and steal their horses. After Smathers was killed, they reckoned to avenge his death by killing my Comanche friend and me. I can show you the bullet holes in our bedrolls. Were it not for Zeb here warning, we'd have been dead bodies wrapped in our blankets. We tracked them and captured the two just east of Fredericksburg. We had to wound them, when they tried to run. So, they have murdered, stolen horses, and attempted murder. Any one of those offenses ought to be punishable by the noose."

"See, Sheriff! They assaulted us," pleaded Tex.

Maier was not to be made a fool of again. He knew that I spoke truthfully despite our personal disagreement over slavery. "Shut up, you fools," he commanded.

Digger and Tex tried to exhibit remorse but to no avail.

"We've got a couple of cells for you two," he stated, then turned to me. "Can you and your Comanche friend hang around for a trial?"

I desperately wanted to get back to Blue Flower. If Lincoln won the election, she could be in danger. "When?"

"You're in luck. The judge is due in town tomorrow."

"We'll stay at the McGregor smithy shop, Sheriff." I gave Digger and Tex and killer look, then turned to the sheriff. "Happy to deposit their horses down at the stable."

"Appreciate that," responded Maier.

In my mind, I calculated that selling the two horses would pay for a hanging and burial. Not a very Christian thought, but God surely approved of punishing the likes of Digger and Tex.

SEVEN
NEW THREATS

WE HUNG with the McGregors for a couple of days and bore witness at the trial. The judge wouldn't permit Spirit Talker to serve as a witness, so I was both accuser and witness in the court's eyes. I must admit that the bedraggled appearance of Digger and Tex didn't help their case. They turned down a court-appointed attorney and ranted wildly, accusing me of entrapping them and denying wrongdoing. They even claimed that we'd assaulted them. Will McGregor and Reggie Wilson took the stand as character witnesses on my behalf. Sheriff Maier was up for reelection, so he testified about the accused men's association with Garth Smathers and the blankets with bullet holes that I'd submitted. It took the jury about fifteen minutes to reach a guilty verdict and another two for the judge to sentence Digger and Tex. Spirit Talker and I watched the two die by the noose the next day. Justice had been served, and it had been swift. I was thankful to my Creator that I had resisted the temptation to take the law into my own hands. Now, Digger and Tex joined Garth Smathers in suffering somewhere in the inferno God reserved for evildoers.

———

THE DAYS WERE GROWING EVER SHORTER. The chill of early November had arrived, but the chill was about more than the weather. The news of Abraham Lincoln's election to the nation's presidency sent a chill over the countryside. Newspapers quickly began blaring talk of southern states seceding from the Union. Spirit Talker and I felt a strong call to return to our families. Uncertain times lay ahead, and our loved ones must be protected.

We bade farewell to the McGregors and Sheriff Maier. I was especially touched by Maier remarking that, while he disagreed with me about slavery, he respected my faith and my courage. That seemed to be a step in the right direction. He even overcame his fears and petted Zeb. And last, he shook Spirit Talker's hand.

McGregor brought our horses from the stable. He and Colleen had given us plenty of jerky and pemmican for our rides back to our homes. *"Vaya con Dios,"* bade McGregor. The Spanish seemed to give a melodic tone to our departure.

I felt a touch of sadness as Spirit Talker and I slowly walked our horses off toward the edge of town. With possible violence looming, Fredericksburg might never be the same.

"Keep Topsannah safe," I cautioned Spirit Talker, as he mounted his pony. Prairie Flower was with child again, so he might be doubly concerned.

"Tosa no bother Penateka, Pohya Isa," he assured me. *"Tosa peeka* each other," he said with a grim smile. He was

right. The Whites would turn their attention to fighting other Whites and not be concerned about the Penateka Comanche or any of the other tribes.

"Worry that Comanche, Kiowa, Apache, and others *peeka tosa*." He held up all his fingers to signify many deaths. The homesteads would be vulnerable to opportunistic tribes looking for revenge over incursions by Whites or simply chances to show their bravery by killing old men and women and stealing horses.

I nodded and mounted Big Red. "Go with God, Mukwooru," I intoned grimly.

Spirit Talker smiled. "Go with God, Pohya Isa. Go with God, Jack O'Toole. Be light in darkness." Heavy words spoken and felt.

We parted ways.

————

I HAD CHOSEN to wear my buckskins, as they afforded me a bit of camouflage in a landscape of orange, brown, and red hues. The streams were mostly dry, so I was glad I'd brought a couple of bota bags full of water. Big Red was especially appreciative during the long ride toward home. We were alone, and folks likely would have thought me crazy at the little conversations I carried on with the big stallion. The lonely ride gave me time to reflect on the five years that had passed since the Comanche massacre at what is now Rising Cross Ranch. I very much missed my ma and pa, though I felt sure they were watching me from Heaven with pride at my survival and accomplishments as a man of faith and purpose. God had surely bestowed strong *sunipu* upon me. Zeb was testament to that. He had become a dutiful and protective companion. While I was concerned, given the rumors floating around about me, the presence of a great wolf served to discourage most troublemakers.

I made camp at what I judged to be about halfway to Rising Cross Ranch. I'd passed the place where the horrors had been inflicted upon Sheesha and Samuel. I even paused to reinter their charred remains and mark the spot with a new cross. It gave me peace of soul.

Despite the brisk air as autumn was delivering its final gasps, I decided to cold camp. There was no point in drawing attention with a fire, and I could chow down on jerky and pemmican. I found an out-of-the-way spot sheltered by an overhanging rock and some scrub brush to spread my bedroll. Between Zeb lying alongside me and the wool blanket Colleen McGregor had gifted me, I'd be plenty warm. I hobbled Big Red behind a stand of oaks. I likely needn't have hobbled him, as he didn't tend to wander.

I slept pretty well far as I could tell. There was a certain peace associated with a wolf lying beside you. I awakened to the jungle of spurs and creaks of leather. I remained motionless but opened my eyes. Three riders passed within twenty feet of my bedroll. They hadn't a clue that I was there. They were a nasty-looking trio carrying enough firepower to start a war.

I overheard tidbits of conversation. There was an apparent effort to recruit a force to do battle with the Northerners and their abolitionist brothers. They had no kind words to say about Abraham Lincoln. In fact, they dreaded his ascension to the presidency. The worst of it was their desire to kill abolitionists.

The three had just about passed on by, when Big Red let out a whinny.

"Hey Burt! Yuh hear that?" exclaimed one of the trio.

I immediately scrambled toward Big Red, keeping low

and screened by as much brush and grasses as were available.

"Yep. Somethin's movin' o'er yonder," observed Burt.

The three riders had stopped, and I could see them animatedly debating whether to investigate.

"I'm gonna check it out," stated one of them finally. "Watch my back."

"You be careful, Slim," came a cautionary voice.

With a mere thirty feet or so for the one man to scout the source of the noise, I reckoned the best defense would be a strong offense. I was tempted to use the Sharps carbine, but it would take time to ready it, and I'd create unwanted noise. I drew out my bow and arrows. I crouched behind a large live oak with low-hanging limbs. I nocked an arrow.

The expression of horror on Slim's face when my six foot plus frame dressed in fringed buckskins rose before him with an arrow aimed at his chest was a sight to behold. It was as though time had frozen. Slim dared not say a word. By now, Zeb had slipped in beside me. The teeth on a full-grown male wolf can have quite an impact on folks he's not friends with.

"Slim, whassup?" came a call from his companions.

I motioned Slim to be quiet and leave.

Slim looked nervously at Zeb. "Nothin', Burt. Just some wild horse passin' through." Slim began to back away, finally walking briskly to his nervous cayuse and mounting up. "Let's be outta here. Place gives me the creeps." The trio rode off slowly without a sound of conversation.

I patted Big Red and ruffled Zeb's mane. Strong *sunipu*, indeed. "Thank you, Lord," I whispered.

———

IT TOOK the better part of the remaining daylight to reach Rising Cross Ranch. I reined in Big Red, pausing to fully take in all that lay before me. Off to my left was my favorite fishing spot. It was where I'd gone, when my pa sent me off to catch some bass for dinner. It all-too-vividly brought back the memory of all my family but Buck and Kate being massacred by Comanche and our cabin burned to the ground. Upon seeing the smoke rising to the skies, I ran as fast as my fifteen-year-old legs could carry me. Alas, I'd be far too late to help. The mix of guilt, anger, vengeance, and despair gnawed at me and tested my faith. But I endured. I discovered true friendship in Spirit Talker, love in Blue Flower and our children, the toughness taught by months among the prairies and mountains of the frontier, the responsibility consequent of running a ranch, a life mission in striving to overcome racial prejudice, and an ever-strengthening faith in God.

The ranch was not only the land, but what we had made of it. Cattle moved before me, chewing on the tall grass like gluttons at some great feast. The stillness was broken by the occasional snort or bellow of a bull or the lowing of a cow. I saw Shorty and Hardy way off in the far north pasture, moving horses. The screech of a hawk pierced the azure sky. Still higher was an eagle floating gracefully on currents as it sought prey. I just sat there on Big Red, taking in God's creation. "What say, big fella? Let's go home," I said with a sigh and nudged the big stallion forward. Zeb trotted behind me with an occasional wary look at the eagle.

Two miles passed in no time. No one was in the yard, so I headed Big Red directly for the barn. The door was open, and I wondered at someone's carelessness. Zeb's ears perked up. I halted and drew my Colt revolver, then peered cautiously into the dimly lit interior. I was met by three sets of eyes framed by dark hair and cheeks decorated with red stripes. Three young Kiowa warriors had Rising Cross Ranch branded horses in tow. They were as surprised as me but had no wolf to warn them and thus failed to arm themselves. From what I gathered, they had seen that no one was visible around the immediate vicinity of the barn. Figuring it was unguarded, they picketed their ponies, stealthily crossed the pasture, snuck into the barn, and reckoned they could spirit away a couple of horses before anyone would catch them. "*Tabu*," I said, figuring they might know the Comanche word for coward. I punctuated that with the click of the hammer pulled back on my Colt.

Outright panic swept their faces. They outnumbered me, but the cold steel in my hands more than made up for numbers. They were young and likely looking to prove themselves by stealing horses. The apparent leader of the trio, the one with more feathers in his hair, gave me a questioning look that combined pride with surrender. They knew their gooses were cooked.

I motioned to return the horses to their stalls which they did with reluctant obedience. Once that was accomplished, I backed Big Red from the barn doorway while motioning them out. Big Red was tall as cowboy cayuses went, so my six-foot-three inches sitting astride him and pointing a gun loaded with six bullets painted a rather imposing threat. The three now stood about twenty feet in front of me. For the moment, we were in a stare-down as I mulled over what to do next with these rascals. Violence would make enemies. I had to think of consequences, think of the future and my earnest desire that all people live in peace. If violence—possibly a war—were to occur, we'd need friends. Out of the corner of my eye, I saw Shorty and Hardy riding in. Time was wasting, if I was going to act.

Imagine the Kiowa surprise, when I holstered my Colt. "No *kooitu* today," I said firmly. It was not their day to die. I motioned them to leave. They unhesitatingly obliged, escaping at a dead run. The leader paused at the corral gate and looked back at me. He made a fist, followed by a peace sign and a finger pointed to the sky. He recognized my strong *sunipu* and would not forget my sparing them.

"Yer back, boss," exclaimed Shorty, as they rode into the yard but seconds after the departing Kiowa.

Having endured the confrontation with Kiowa but moments earlier, my response was low-key. "Yep, I'm home."

They followed me into the barn. Shorty dismounted and gazed at the stalls. "Who switched them hosses around?"

I shook my head. If only he knew. I didn't figure to tell him, as I didn't want them taking off after the young Kiowa warriors.

Shorty gave me an appreciative look. I'd been away for a couple of weeks. "I'll take care of Big Red, boss. You go see Blue Flower."

I appreciated his thoughtfulness. "It's good to be home. Tell you all about it later." With that, I headed to the house. As I approached the door, I could hear Blue Flower in the kitchen. I was surprised that the jingle of my spurs and the thud of my boots on the wooden gallery hadn't given me away. Pausing for a second, I pushed the door open and tossed my saddlebags toward the center of the room.

Blue Flower let out a startled squeal followed by a joyous shout, as she realized who belonged to the saddlebags. She flew into my waiting arms, nearly bowling me over. "Jack! Jack! Jack!" she cried out, burying her face in my chest. Isa, George, and Peter looked curiously for a second then toddled to my feet, while baby Nadua was oblivious to my arrival. "*Kamakuna,*" cooed Blue Flower. Her loving husband was home safe and sound.

I said nothing but simply enjoyed the moment. There would be plenty of challenges ahead but nothing would disturb the peace of this very point in time. I held her tightly for what seemed an eternity. Only Nadua's plaintive hunger cry caused us to pull apart.

Blue Flower took hold of my arm and guided us to a newly acquired settee. She picked up Nadua and nursed while I sat quietly with my arm around her. She was more beautiful than ever, as she nestled against me.

"Jack home. Stay." I assured her.

She looked up at me with the same smile that captured my heart years ago.

Our peace was broken by Isa and George clamoring for attention. "Pa?" asked George.

"They talk now," said Blue Flower. "I tell of return of their pa."

It surprised me that she hadn't taught them the Comanche word for father: *ap*. I swept the twins up into my arms while Peter tried to climb my leg. The whole family was now clustered around the settee. I gazed lovingly at my young sons. We had managed to find books from which we did our best to teach them of the world. We made great use of the near dog-eared copy of the Bible that George Freeman had given me. That reminiscence caused me to recall the Bible that had saved my life by stopping a bullet meant for my heart. Isa, George, and Peter would soon enough be learning ways of the world that would never be found in any books. There was no substitute for hands-on learning on the frontier.

"*Ana o'a hi'it?*" asked Blue Flower.

Indeed, I was hungry. There'd be plenty of time for romancing and for telling about my adventures.

Blue Flower placed Nadua in the cradleboard, smiled lovingly at me and our boys, and headed for the kitchen.

With food appearing on the kitchen table, the boys answered the lure of their mother's cooking and bolted headlong for their seats. I watched them fondly for a moment as they climbed into their chairs and followed. Joy filled my heart. It was good to be home.

Blue Flower sat in the chair beside me. We joined hands, blessed the meal, and began eating. The boys made great use of their fingers in tearing apart meat and stuffing pieces of potato in their mouths. They'd learn the knife and fork soon enough. In the Comanche culture, women held responsibility for educating the boys until they became old enough to hunt. At that time, usually around ten or eleven years old, they fell under the guidance of the men. It seemed quite sensible to me.

"Lincoln was elected president," I said matter-of-factly, as I scooped a spoonful of peas. "News has it that South Carolina is voting to leave the nation."

"Leave nation?" asked Blue Flower. "Like Penateka leave Quahadi?"

"Well, the United States is a nation divided into states that agreed to follow a constitution that provides over-arching law guiding our republic. The Comanche have no such document. Leaving the Union is called secession. South Carolina is seceding."

"What about Texas?" she asked. Blue Flower was quick to draw a link given what we'd endured concerning our own beliefs about slavery and the conversations she'd listened in on about popular sovereignty.

I knew where the political sway resided, it was with the powerful slaveholders. With the growth of Rising Cross Ranch, our influence had grown but was still dwarfed by the plantation owners. The politicians in Austin leaned toward the money that kept them in power and wouldn't be giving a listen to folks like me. Cattlemen had no need for slaves, yet slavery and slave-holders were galvanizing the state toward following in South Carolina's footsteps. "I hear that Governor Houston supports slavery but is against leaving the Union," I remarked. "They reckon to call the new government the Confederate States of America. Once secession gets rolling, all the southern states will climb aboard." I shook my head resignedly.

Blue Flower's face was about as seriously fearful as I'd ever seen. "What of us, Jack?"

"I expect this Lincoln fellow won't cotton to states leaving the Union. He'll do anything to keep the country together. Emotions are high, and that means there may be war. If that happens, they'll be forming armies."

"Jack join army?"

My eyes took in Blue Flower and our children. "I will not fight against the United States."

"People make trouble for us," Blue Flower stated flatly.

I nodded. "There could be trouble, and we must be ready."

"What about…" Her voice trailed off.

I interrupted. "Will and Kate, Isaac and Sarah, Buck, our ranch hands…all must decide where they stand. We can defend Rising Cross if necessary." I took a deep breath. "We will not run from this."

Blue Flower smiled. "Jack warrior. Jack strong *sunipu*."

I was blessed with a strong woman who fully believed in me. As if on cue, Zeb eased over and proceeded to nuzzle Isa and George. They giggled with delight, as they were too young to be fearful of the great wolf.

As I understood it influence is a combination of communicating and persuading to have an impact on thinking, character development, and conduct. Particular circumstances, such as prejudice, slavery, or warfare, defined the levels of influence. I believed that God had chosen me to be an influencer. I would not be seduced by the sort of powers that led to secession. I had faith that by following God's laws, all would ultimately turn out well. In addition to stepping up to defend my family and beliefs, I was determined to aggressively influence those whom I could. I reckoned to send letters to northern newspapers that spoke out against slavery and support for the Union. Hopefully, some would be published and give folks hope for a peaceful future. I was no fool. I'd use a fictitious name, an alias, to protect my family.

Still, I had to face reality. There were new threats to deal with.

EIGHT
WAR!

TIME HAD SEEMED TO FLY. Christmas raced past, and we were soon into the new year. It was already the end of January. Blessedly, we'd encountered no problems with neighbors, even though they were well aware of our stance on slavery. That likely wouldn't last much longer. I'd received word that Sam Houston had been ousted from the governorship due to his unionist leanings, and Lieutenant Governor Edward Clark installed. A Secession Convention was assembled and Ordinances of Secession introduced. They were expected to pass overwhelmingly. Once passed, there'd be a referendum of the citizens of Texas. Again, secession was likely to pass.

I brought together my family, the Fishers, and our ranch hands to discuss the looming threat of war and what role Rising Cross Ranch might play. Clouds off to the northwest threatened harsh weather, as we gathered around a roaring fire at the hearth in our house. Blue Flower and Kate served up coffee, and Perez doled out some snacks he called tacos. Everyone was in good spirits despite the serious nature of what we'd be discussing.

"Dang Juan, you been holding out on us with these taco things," crooned Hardy.

Perez basked in his taco glory until Blue Flower brought out the bear sign. The electable sweet treats had it hands down over a tortilla shell filled with meat, lettuce, tomatoes, and jalapeño peppers. Perez proceeded to alternately bite a taco and a bear sign, laughing between chews. At least our beloved Mexican cook's mirth was infectious despite the grom topic for which we assembled.

I shoved another log onto the fire and scanned the gathering. Everyone was here. I hoped and prayed we'd all be here when the looming hostilities ended. My roaming across the frontier over the past few years had necessarily faded into a memorable background as a new threat was faced. I cleared my throat. "I expect y'all understand what we're going to talk about."

Heads nodded.

I explained what was going on with the legislature. "South Carolina has seceded along with Mississippi, Florida, Alabama, Georgia, and Louisiana. Texas will soon follow. Fearing an uprising, a Major Anderson moved his troops from Fort Moultrie to the more defensible Fort Sumter. South Carolina seized Fort Johnson in Charleston Harbor and threatens Fort Sumter. An attack would ignite a war. Forts have been seized throughout the South. Men are being recruited to flesh out state militias. Emotions have heated to a fever pitch." I looked at Blue Flower, and she nodded approval. I was now looking at a sea of grim-looking faces. Half-eaten tacos and bear sign lay on folks' plates.

"The lingering question is what we will do here at Rising Cross Ranch. First, let me be clear that y'all know where I stand on slavery. I won't hold it against any man who leaves to join this new Confederacy thing they're talking about." I looked around the room. Will, Buck, Isaac, and the hands were looking at me as though wondering how I could possibly think they'd leave. They were loyal to the Union. "If y'all decide to stay, we might be forced to defend against attack."

I saw collective nods. "Indians may also attack. With able-bodied men called away to serve in militias, defenses will be weakened and the tribes will grow bold in their overconfidence. We have both friends and enemies among the Comanche and Kiowa, but we dare not be careless. There will be evil White men who will try to take advantage of our perceived weaknesses. War or not, we're going to have to move cattle to market this year, and that will leave Rising Cross vulnerable. The main house is like a fortress and offers our best defense." I paused to let that sink in. "We'll keep plenty of loaded arms handy. If we must go to Fredericksburg for supplies, we will travel at night to minimize being discovered."

"Loved yer tacos, Juan," said Shorty with a chuckle that broke the deadly silence painted across the room.

———

TEXAS IS a big place and its frontier is sparsely settled despite being home to more than half a million humans. Anything approaching civilization for us was a ride of at least two days. Bandera, Uvalde, Fredericksburg, pretty much any place there were some shops, a church, maybe a one-room school, a jail, and a stable could be considered civilization. Anyone looking to make trouble with Rising Cross Ranch would have to go out of their way. If there was more than a handful, it was likely they'd be spotted before they got close.

We rolled into winter with no trouble here at the ranch. At the Texas State Convention on February 1st, the vote to secede was 166 to 7. It was ratified by public referendum three weeks later. The die was cast.

Sam Johnson, Collins's foreman at the nearby Circle C, stopped by on his way back from Bandera for supplies. He intercepted me as I was saddling up Big Red for a ride out to the north pastures. "Howdy, Jack!" he called just as I was ready to mount up.

"Hank. Good to see you," I responded in anticipation of news. "What's happening in Bandera?" I stole a glance at his wagon and gave a friendly nod to the driver. I noted that it wasn't so full as normal.

Johnson shook his head. "Nothin' good. Supplies are bein' hoarded. Folks are on edge. They're askin' fer volunteers, but they'll be recruitin' afore long."

"You figure to join up?"

"Got cattle to tend to. We raise an army, it's gotta be fed. Not sure 'bout our other hands."

"What's that thing hanging off the back of the seat?"

Johnson chuckled. "They be callin' it the Texas Battle Flag. I ain't takin' it serious." His face grew grim. "Figger if we fly the thing, they be leavin' us be."

"Thanks for stopping by. Help yourself to some coffee. Blue Flower has some brewing."

"Appreciate it, Jack, but I'll be movin' on."

I watched Johnson and the accompanying wagon roll on away and mounted up. Hardy joined me. As I'd advised everyone, we always ventured out in pairs. Zeb gave us an extra edge.

———

WITH APRIL'S ARRIVAL, war finally arrived. We'd learned the Sumter news that morning from a traveler passing on through. I got the impression that the young man was trying to avoid involvement in the coming conflict. We wished him luck, as he headed westward.

I found myself on the south range with Shorty rounding up strays. The bluebonnets were in full bloom, painting the landscape in swaths of vibrant blue. Despite the threat of conflict, I found that the gentle rolling hills of Rising Cross tended to soothe the soul.

"What do yuh think, boss?" asked Shorty, as he nudged a cow along. "Kin the Rebs win?"

"I don't see how the Confederacy can win."

"Why say yuh that?" he responded.

"The Union has far more resources. There'll be plenty of fighting mind you, but it'll be more a war of attrition. The South will run out of men, supplies, and the will to fight. It won't be pretty, Shorty."

"Dang, but that makes sense, boss." He shook his head. "How long yuh think it'll take?"

I nodded grimly. "Fighting won't go more than a couple of years. Three at most. It's going to set Texas back economically for quite a spell. Worse, lots of fine men are going to die. The good Lord is going to have lots of folks lined up at the Pearly Gates up yonder in Heaven." I scanned the thick brush and tall grasses around us. "Life can be hard. We've got to be tough."

"Think we can outlast 'em at Rising Cross?" Shorty asked.

"Do we have a choice?" I responded. "Hey there!" My attention was diverted by a maverick off in a stand of grass. I spurred Big Red to corral the beast. It swung its great horns at us, but Big Red was too savvy for that maneuver and side-stepped deftly out of range.

We gathered about a dozen beeves and headed them northward.

NINE
VIGILANTE REPRISE

THE WEATHER WAS HEATING UP. It felt more like summer than spring. Shorty and I left the beeves in a south pasture a bit closer to our main ranch buildings. We were beginning to seriously consider a trail drive, though it remained to be seen who we would sell our cattle to. We rode up to the barn to settle our horses before turning them loose among the mares.

Work done and stomach growling for Blue Flower's fine cooking, I turned to head for the house. I almost knocked Blue Flower clean over, managing to scoop her up before she fell.

"Blue Flower like," she cooed with a come-on smile, as I held her close.

"I'll be moseying," said an embarrassed Shorty.

I set her on her feet.

"Hear you ride in," said Blue Flower. She waved a letter at me. It looked like George Freeman's scrawl on the envelope.

"Anything new?" I asked,

"They have baby. Name Abraham in honor of new president." She handed the envelope to me.

I slipped the letter out, unfolded it, and read the news for myself. George said that Fort Laramie was being garrisoned by volunteer troops because regular troops were sent east. He also noted that the Northern Cheyenne and Oglala Lakota were especially restless. Indian Agent Thomas Twiss was at his wit's end trying to keep the peace. Other than a brief mention of most of their cattle and horses surviving the winter and having added a bedroom to their cabin, I sensed that he and Running Waters were cautiously optimistic that they would weather any hostilities.

"Ana o'a hi'it?"

Yes, I was hungry.

Blue Flower latched onto my elbow and began pulling me toward the house.

I tried to look helpless, as Hardy, Will, and Buck rode in from patrolling the northern range. My humor was swept away by the sight of a dozen riders about a quarter mile off and heading our way. The dust cloud told me that they were riding hard. "Men! We're about to have company !" I shook loose of Blue Flower and pointed. "Alert Shorty and Perez in the bunkhouse and let Isaac know." I didn't have a good feeling about our unexpected visitors. "Gather back at the house." Our house was designed to double as a fortress, so it was a natural place from which to defend ourselves. "Don't stick any guns from the ports until we find out what they're looking for." There was no point in provoking any gunplay.

It took a couple of minutes for the riders to arrive, but they did so with considerable fanfare. I recognized Rowdy Sikes out front, and he looked ready to take on the world. "O'Toole!" he called out. "You ready to come to Austin an' join up?"

I stood with my hands clear of my weapons. Everyone could see that I wasn't looking for trouble. "What you joining, Rowdy?" I tried to sound friendly and even a bit enthusiastic. I knew him as a cowhand who was about average with his skills and did odd ranch jobs when there wasn't a trail drive to join.

"An army is formin' up, O'Toole. Everybody's joinin'." He insisted.

I counted twelve riders with him. They all appeared to be sharing Sikes's aim to join a newly-forming Confederate army. "I'll ask my hands, Rowdy." With that, I poked my head inside our house, waited a few seconds, and then turned back to Sikes. "No takers here," I said straightforwardly. "Somebody's got to stay back and feed the army, Rowdy. Y'all go on and fight those Yankees folks are talking about." I recognized the horses of a couple of the men Sikes had riding with him. They'd been among the vigilantes who'd tried to lynch me as an abolitionist. I saw them throw some barely audible words at Sikes.

"You ain't fallen back on yer abolition ways, have yuh, O'Toole?"

Knowing the weapons backing me up, I felt a bit more confident than I should have. I reckoned God being on my side gave me an edge, though I doubt that He was big on foolish choices. "Y'all looking to try to string me up again?" I challenged. "Told y'all that I'm raising cattle to sell to the highest bidder. That includes the Confederate army, if it pays in gold." I was making no bones as to my intentions. War or not, I was a rancher and in the business to make money.

There were more murmurs among the interlopers. A

couple appeared to be itching to take me on. "I can hold 'em back just so long, O'Toole," advised Sikes.

I finally had to play my ace card. "You're a smart enough man to know what 50 caliber bullets can do to a human body, Rowdy. Right now, there's a half dozen Sharps carbines pointed your way. When the blood-letting's done, I'll let Zeb here and his pack chew on whatever' left of y'all." I wasn't exactly showing Christian love, but I reckoned my warning was the right thing given the circumstances. Evil acts would be punished. I raised my hand, and every gun port in the house sported a large-bore muzzle.

The men with Sikes began to look furtively at each other and back their horses away. "That yer final decision, O'Toole?" Sikes tried to maintain his grip on leading his rabble. "We'll give yuh time to reflect."

I nodded. "You do that, Rowdy. And when your men are hungry, they just might be chowing down on my beeves."

Sikes snorted and led his men off at a gallop.

I shook my head.

Blue Flower and the others emerged from the house.

TEN
HOME DEFENSE

WORDS CAN TRAVEL like a prairie fire in a strong wind. This day was no exception. News reached us that troops of the Confederacy had fired upon Fort Sumter in South Carolina. We were at war. Some called it a civil war, but I could imagine nothing civil about it.

Spring was usually a time of renewal at Rising Cross Ranch, but the stories beginning to reach us took an edge from the exhilaration of newborn calves and foals, buds sprouting from early spring plantings, and repair of winter-beaten buildings and fences.

I was mending the gate to the corral alongside the barn, when Sam Collins rode in and pulled up in a cloud of dust.

"Howdy, Jack," he greeted with an upbeat tone. He alighted from his horse and strode over to the corral.

"Welcome, friend," I responded and shook his hand. Zeb knew him as a friend and trotted over to give Collins's hand a thorough licking.

As he viewed Zeb's massive teeth, Collins must have wondered what it was like for an enemy to feel the wolf's wrath. He tousled Zeb's mane and looked over at me. "Hear tell the Federals took a licking at a place in Virginia called Manassas. Looks like we're actually at war." He shook his head with dismay.

I took a deep breath. "Hold this a second, Sam." I finished securing the gate hinge while Collins held it in place. "Going to be a bunch of folks killed and wounded before it's all over," I observed.

"Circle C already lost two hands to the army," lamented Sam.

We looked knowingly at each other. An extended war could be devastating to all that had been built in Texas, in the nation, for that matter. "The politicians keep talking about popular sovereignty like it was an elixir for some sort of malady. I think the malady is in men's hearts."

Blue Flower emerged from our house and headed our way with two cups of coffee in hand. She gave Collins a welcoming smile. "*Ana o'a hi'it?*" she asked.

Collins had heard the Comanche invitation to eat before. "*Tosa ana o'a hi'it.*" He responded.

We'd be having a guest for dinner. Collins was a good storyteller, so Isa and George would fully enjoy his company. Peter was yet too young to understand, and Nadua still suckled at Blue Flower's breast.

I didn't know how Blue Flower managed it all. Four young children, a house to maintain, garden to tend, butter to churn, hides to tan, the tasks seemed endless. She was intelligent, fearless, and a passionate lover. I boasted that she could shoot the tail off a leaping grasshopper. She took pride in her appearance. In Blue Flower, God had gifted me with the most beautiful woman on earth.

"Sam have new *wa'ipu?*" she asked Collins, as he bit into a thick piece of steak.

Collins nodded as he chewed. "Yep. Meant to tell y'all." He turned to Blue Flower. "How'd you know?"

"*Wa'ipu* know." She said confidently.

"Well, we're expecting a child," added Collins.

Blue Flower smiled as though she knew that as well. Apparently, words of war weren't the only news that traveled the prairies.

"Anyone pressed you to join the Rebels, Sam?"

"Not yet, but it'll come sure as rain."

Blue Flower shot me a *let's not talk about war* look. She might have been raised as a Comanche, but she was a wife and mother first and foremost. She'd seen bloodied warriors return from battle, endured kidnapping by a rogue Lakota, shared my passions against racial and cultural prejudices, and now sought a bit of relief from the worries of war.

I didn't have to be hinted at twice. "Congratulations, Sam. We hope and pray y'all have a healthy baby."

Collins had seen Blue Flower's look and picked up on my shift in conversation. "Martha seems to be doing great. You know how hard women around these parts work no matter whether they're with child."

We scraped every morsel from our plates and figured we were finished, when Blue Flower brought out a cherry pie. It struck me that right now, at this very moment, we were experiencing about as much of what might be called normalcy as we might expect for some time to come. We were in a constant struggle to seek an ever-better life, a life as God would have us live. Change was a constant, and that meant constant adaptation.

Collins scarfed down a last bite of pie and turned to George and Isa. "Did I ever tell you boys about my run-in with the grizzly bear?" He went on to entertain the twins for the next half hour.

After thanking Blue Flower, Collins followed me out to the barn where Buck had already saddled his horse. "Thanks again, Jack, for the dinner. I'll have to bring Martha next time." He paused. I knew there was more on his mind.

"What's sticking in your craw, Sam?" I asked.

"The Army of the Confederacy must be fed. I heard from ranchers down in Bandera that they're getting paid with script. If the South loses, that paper won't be worth wiping your rear end with."

"Nobody taking a stand for payment in gold?" I ventured.

"What gold?" replied Collins.

"I've got a cousin John Dunn talking about running cotton down to Vera Cruz for the Rebels. I expect he'll face the same issue as to payment."

"The powerful politicians in Austin been running their mouths about how they're going to put a whipping on those Yankees. Mark my words, Jack, they might have some early victories, but we both know the North has far greater resources to wage war."

"You thinking what I'm thinking about where to sell our beeves?"

Collins pointed northward.

"It'll make it interesting, when Rebel foragers nose around and wonder why we're not selling out cattle to the Confederacy." I gave a rueful shake of my head. "In fact, it could get nasty around here."

"Hope your home doesn't have to serve as the fortress y'all built it to be," he said with an ironic grimace.

"I expect we'll have a good-sized herd ready by next spring to drive north, Sam. You're welcome to join us."

"Much obliged, Jack. Expect I'll take you up on that." Collins mounted, tipped his hat, and rode off.

"What's goin' on?" asked Shorty, as he emerged from the barn.

"Fixing to mount a drive northward next spring. It'll be great to see George again," I responded. Between the Circle C and us, we ought to put together better than five hundred head."

"You fixin' to sell hosses to the Rebs, boss?"

By this time, Buck, Hardy, and Will had joined the impromptu gathering.

"Good question, Shorty. Horses might be our salvation, if foragers come snooping. The cavalry is always looking for good horseflesh, and ours are among the best to be had. Shucks, I think only the King Ranch might have better."

"You fearing problems, big brother?" Buck asked from where he sat on the top rail of the corral. He'd grown a couple of inches since way back when we rescued him and Kate from the Comanche and was nearly as tall as me.

I nodded. "With a war beginning to rage, we're going to have to be more alert than ever. The Confederacy will try to recruit, maybe even force men to join up. More troubling is the threat of Indians taking advantage of men folk having gone off to fight. Ranches, farms, and even towns will be vulnerable. God has blessed us, but there may yet be violence ahead."

"How about the Mexicans?" asked Hardy.

"Hopefully, we're far enough north of the border to be clear of their *Guerra de Reforma*," I postulated. "I expect we can sit back while Benito Juarez and Ignacio Comonfort sort things out."

The men nodded agreement.

"As Shorty and I were saying, we'll plan on a drive north next spring. Meanwhile, keep your ears to the ground for signs of trouble. Y'all know we're already on their nasty list for my expressed opposition to slavery. Some would love an excuse to make trouble." I looked from face-to-face. "I think we all have chores to do before that sun up yonder sets." I walked into the barn to muck stalls.

———

I HEARD them coming before I saw them. The August heat was already causing sweat to soak our clothes. This visit was happening sooner than expected. I looked over and motioned to Blue Flower to ring the iron dinner bell. Our hands would all know what to do. Zeb's ear perked up.

Twelve of them reined in with a huge cloud of dust and a jingle of spurs and sabers. They were clothed in a motley assortment of gray uniforms. But the leader was impeccably dressed in officer's trappings. It was quite clear that some money had been spent to outfit him properly.

"Captain Anthony Pedigrew at your service, sir," stated the officer with a snappy salute.

I tipped back my hat and took a long look at the captain and his modest command. What was a captain doing leading a foraging party? I didn't get the sense that one of them could effectively wield a saber in battle. These would be foragers, not men destined for the front lines of battle—yet. "My name is Jack O'Toole. I own this spread," I responded all cool, calm, and collected. "May I be of service?"

"Thank you, Mr. O'Toole. We understand that you raise a fine stock of horseflesh, sir. We seek to purchase a dozen of your finest."

Pedigrew got down to business right quickly. There were no social niceties to be had. "Nice day, captain. Care to set a spell?" I reckoned I'd make an effort to be hospitable.

"Thank you, Mr. O'Toole, but we must be on our way." Pedigrew seemed distracted, though it wasn't clear what caused it.

"What are you offering, captain?" I asked.

Pedigrew looked as though he wasn't prepared to make an offer. Apparently, he had it figured that I'd set a price. "Er...seventy-five dollars, sir."

I shook my head. "We typically get about a hundred twenty-five dollars a head for our prime horses, captain. Are you paying with gold?" I could get down to the bottom line right-quickly myself.

Pedigrew gave me a curious look. "Confederate script is backed by gold, sir."

"Perhaps the captain would care to dismount and inspect a few of the horses we have over in yonder corral," I said while pointing to a couple of our lesser-quality horses in the smaller corral alongside the barn. I suspected that Captain Pedigrew wasn't a skilled negotiator of livestock.

The captain dismounted with a show of saber rattling. "Watch after my mount, sergeant."

A grizzled older trooper in a dirty gray uniform with a trio of stripes on his sleeve rode forward and took the reins of the captain's horse.

The captain followed me to the corral. "Y'all seen any battle yet?" I ventured.

Now, out of hearing of his men, Pedigrew was a tad more relaxed. "I'm expecting orders to head to the Rio Grande and report to Lieutenant Colonel John Baylor for a campaign into New Mexico Territory."

I had heard some talk about Baylor. He'd gained the surrender of federal troops in San Antonio and was given command of the Western Frontier under Colonel Rip Ford. Of greater interest to me was that Baylor had enjoyed considerable success defending Texans against Comanche for several years prior to the war. In fact, he'd led a party of four men that killed thirteen warriors and took back fifty horses the hostiles had stolen in Palo Pinto County. I gave Pedigrew an appraising once over. Money had purchased his commission and fancy uniform. I doubted that he'd be the caliber to fight alongside Baylor. "Where are you from, captain?" I asked as I led him through the corral gate.

"Galveston, sir," he responded while inspecting a gelding I'd led over to him.

"I guess you heard that Lieutenant Colonel Baylor captured Mesilla in eastern New Mexico and claimed possession of the territory for the Confederacy."

Pedigrew puffed his chest a bit. "Yes sir, I'm sure proud to be fighting for the Confederate States of America." He patted the gelding's withers, then flinched when the horse whinnied loudly.

"Right nice horse," he said in an effort to cover his reaction.

"Your man Baylor went about dismantling Yankee forts, leaving the territory vulnerable. The Apache have quickly taken advantage." My comment seemed to slide over Pedigrew's head. In any case, his appraising one of my lesser-quality cayuses as right nice didn't surprise me. I reckoned this was an opportunity to divest a dozen of my older, less-than-prime horses. "I'll take no less than a hundred dollars a head, captain." I hoped I'd be able to turn over the Confederate script quickly, so as not to lose too much on the sale.

"You've got a deal, Mr. O'Toole," responded the captain.

I held back a triumphant smile. It wasn't the Christian thing to gloat. "I'll get my cowboys to gather a dozen for you, captain." I shook his hand. "Perhaps, you'd enjoy some coffee while we wait?"

The captain ordered the sergeant to have the men dismount and be at ease. They proceeded to water their horses and drink a bit themselves.

I took Shorty aside and shared the situation, especially that we were being paid with money of doubtful value. He and Will rode out to round up another eleven of our lesser-quality stock to add to the gelding in the corral. Meanwhile, I excused myself, poked my head in our front door, and asked Blue Flower to brew up some coffee.

A few minutes later, she emerged with a pot of coffee in hand, along with a couple of cups.

Upon seeing Blue Flower, Pedigrew stood back with a surprised expression across his face. He turned abruptly to me. "You keeping one of those savage squaws to serve you, sir?"

It would have been easy, even natural, to take umbrage with the captain's remark. "Blue Flower is my wife, captain," I stated unequivocally. "She's the daughter of Comanche Chief Buffalo Hump."

"Hrumph!" grumbled Pedigrew. "Didn't know we were dealing with an Indian lover."

I struggled to hold back my anger. "I've had my share of fighting Indians from here to Nebraska Territory, Captain Pedigrew. I scouted for Texas Ranger Captain Ford at the Battle of Little Robe Creek. My choice of spouse has nothing to do with the fact that she's an Indian, sir. She's the loving mother to our four children." I wanted to say that she'd take his scalp in a heartbeat. "Now, do you still want to purchase my horses, captain?"

About this time, Pedigrew noticed Zeb. "That a wolf?" he asked nervously.

It was pretty danged obvious that Zeb was no domesticated dog. "Zeb here is kind of attached to me," I responded. Zeb trotted over beside me, and I ruffled his mane.

Shorty and Will came riding in with the horses, driving them into the corral.

With his prejudice having come clear over Blue Flower's heritage, the appearance of Zeb, and now the horses, Pedigrew became quite disconcerted. He fished in his bag and pulled out a bundle of Confederate script. He made a quick count and handed it to me. "Sergeant, mount up. Let's move out," he ordered.

I didn't bother to count the money. I just breathed a sigh of good riddance.

Shorty and Will helped the Rebels gather the horses from the corral and headed them on their way.

"Safe travels, captain," I offered as he moved out with the horses. If he heard me, I was ignored.

The Rebel foragers were no sooner out of sight, and we'd begun to have a laugh at having disposed of some of our less-than-sellable horses, when a shot rang out from the north side of the barn. Bullets whizzed over our heads and into the dirt around us, as we bolted for the house. We all made it unscathed and were pleased to find

Blue Flower unharmed and already closing the gun ports and placing loaded rifles alongside them.

I took a gander through a port. There were six of what appeared to be young Noconi Comanche warriors. They had managed to get hold of a bunch of old Springfield rifled muskets and were using them—blessedly—to ill effect.

As the muzzles of our Sharps carbines poked through the gun ports, I hoped the hostiles would see them and take flight. The very thought of killing these misguided young warriors intent on first coups was anathema to me. I looked over my shoulder at Shorty, Will, and Perez, each manning a port while Blue Flower protected our children. "Let's see if we can discourage them," I said. "Hold your fire."

A bullet struck the port I was looking from, and an exploded splinter scratched my forehead. I sighed and aimed mt Sharps through the same port. Maybe I could just wound one. I aimed at a charging warrior that appeared to be the leader, squeezed my trigger, and hit him full on dead center in his chest. So much for wounding the attackers.

My shot brought the band to a halt, as they rode off to reconsider their attack. About this time, Buck and Hardy rode in. Having heard the shooting, they galloped in with guns blazing.

I threw open the front door and stepped onto the gallery. "Cease fire!" I shouted to Buck and Hardy. "No *peeka numunuu*, strong *sunipu!*" I hoped that my mix of English and Comanche would reach the Noconi and defuse the situation. I told them to stop killing the people and that they faced strong medicine. A quiet settled over the scene.

One of the warriors, braver than the others, stepped from cover. "Isananika," he said, pointing to his chest.

His name translated to Howling Wolf.

"Pohya Isa," I replied, pointing to myself.

Howling Wolf signed that he wished to retrieve the body of the fallen warrior.

I joined my hands across my chest in a sign of peace and motioned him forward.

Howling Wolf dismounted, scanned his surroundings, and tentatively walked over to the warrior's body. He made a motion to his scalp as though wondering why I had not taken the dead man's hair.

I pointed skyward. *"Taa Narumi."* The warrior's soul could go to his spirit world.

The Noconi Comanche warrior responded with a satisfied expression and carried his brother away.

I hoped my compassion would not go unappreciated. Hopefully, it would discourage their fellows from trying to prove themselves against the strong *sunipu* of Rising Cross Ranch. I motioned everyone to relax, as the Comanche rode off. Howling Wolf would likely tell others of the White man's largesse, especially that of Walks With Wolves.

It had been quite a morning, what with the Confederate foragers, followed by the Comanche raid. I prayed to my Lord that it wouldn't be repeated any time soon.

ELEVEN
MANIFEST CHAOS

IT WAS time for me to get on with my plan to send letters to Northern newspapers about how we who opposed slavery were managing to survive while living in the midst of enemy territory. My hope was to motivate them to endure, to carry the fight.

There was no way to make multiple copies of anything I wrote, so I decided to write my letters to the largest newspaper I could find. It took a trip to the library in Austin to settle on the *New York Tribune*. In perusing its tattered pages, I found that it had a broad reach. Shucks, copies had even made their way to Texas.

Whoever coined the phrase *war is hell* was a master of understatement. One of Collins's hands returned to the Circle C in the fall, having lost part of one arm. Once he'd recovered, I was amazed at how well the man could throw a lasso. Even with one arm, he was a productive working cowboy.

One evening just before Christmas and Buck and Hardy had returned from a trip to Bandera for supplies, we gathered around the hearth to hear what they'd learned of the war. Notably, we had re-established a working relationship with August Klappenbach, as nearly all the men who'd caused trouble over slavery had joined the Rebel cause. They told of the Battle of Bull Run, where Confederate forces routed the Yankees, and General Jackson received his nickname: *Stonewall*. The Rebels put a whipping on Union forces at the Battle of Lexington in Missouri and the Battle of Ball's Bluff in Virginia. I found it curious that none of the Union victories were mentioned, though they did lament the defeat of J.E.B. Stuart at Dranesville, Virginia. All-in-all, the conduct of the war seemed chaotic. I prayed it would end sooner than later.

In a writing frenzy stirred by my fears of an extended war, I wrote a dozen letters to the *Tribune*. I won't share them all, but one follows that I wrote one night by candlelight while Blue Flower and our children slept:

Dear Yankee,

It is said that a man without hope is dead. So too with freedom.

There are men here in Texas who yearn to be free of the yoke of Southern oppression that would enslave men to their will. This tyranny of the soul oppresses some men physically by enslavement and others mentally by force of threatened harm.

John 8:33 tells us that we are set free by truth. We who carry the burden in Texas seek freedom by sustaining God's truth. We resist the evil influences of those who would punish us for our belief in the cause of the Union. We trust in the Lord and not the wayward opinions of those who would destroy our nation.

Carry on the cause of a unified nation free of slavery. Let not popular sovereignty be a ruse to camouflage the sins of enslavement. Let the pursuit of life, liberty, and happiness be at hand for all men no matter the color of their skin.

Fight on and may victory be ours.

Blessedly,
Zebediah Smith.

The name I signed was fictitious, of course, with apologies to my wolf companion, Zeb. I was concerned that a letter to a New York newspaper might not make it out of Texas. The last thing I needed was for one of my letters to be opened and somehow traced back to me. My letters were posted to my good friend George Freeman, who was able to post them from nearby Fort Laramie. I could only hope that they eventually reached the *Tribune*.

————

WE SURVIVED the winter into 1862 with no further contact by foragers, recruiters, or Indians. I held high hopes that we'd muster a goodly herd to drive northward once the cold weather broke. We did get word from Collins that Martha had delivered a baby boy. He was a button-busting, proud papa.

I decided it was time for me to venture back to Bandera. It had been many months since threats had discouraged me, and I rather missed chatting with my old friend August Klappenbach. Upon considerable reflection and Blue Flower's considerable influence, it was decided that the three of us would make the journey. Since it was an exploratory trip to get a feel for war sentiment, we reckoned to leave the wagon at the ranch. It gave us considerably greater flexibility to not be slowed by a lumbering buckboard that made every creek or river crossing an adventure unto itself. Moreover, if we encountered trouble, we were far more mobile.

Was it a sign that Zeb appeared with his pack? He was accompanied by eight wolves. Far as I could tell, they ranged in age from two to four years. One male was nearly as big as Zeb.

Blue Flower's soft lips broke into one of her beautiful smiles as I prepared to mount up with Buck and Hardy. "Go with God," came her earnest plea, as she hugged me tight and gave me a kiss I wouldn't soon forget. We'd been married for five years, and our times together were as filled with love as our first days as newlyweds. Isa, George, and Peter waved from the gallery while Nadua slept in her cradleboard.

I wore my buckskins to better blend with the landscape between Rising Cross Ranch and Bandera. We'd be traveling across wide grassy expenses at first, then plunge into the southern hills and a couple of crossings of the Medina River. I brought my trusty Sharps carbine, newly purchased Colt 1860 Army Revolver, Bowie knife, and my bow and arrows. Some of the habits I'd picked up from my Comanche brother Spirit Talker had caught on with hands around the Rising Cross Ranch. Buck and Hardy both wore buckskin shirts, and Hardy had learned to fashion his own bow and arrows as a hobby. But for the cowboy tack on our horses and our hats and boots, we'd be looking like an Indian hunting party.

I found myself quite taken with how my life had been shaped, since the loss of most of my family at the hands of a Comanche war party. Each of us grows in our own unique way, like the various blades of grass, colorful petals of flowers, or wind-twisted outreach of tree limbs. I was a man steeped in God's ways, but a man nevertheless. I had come to accept the challenge, the joys, the very wonders of God's creation and taken it to my bones. I believed that the glory of God was only found in men fully alive. Jesus wanted man to thrive, and I would not be one to deny His wishes. I sought the best life, so I could share it with those around me. Yet, there was much to learn. I didn't know how much I didn't know, and therein was my challenge. It drove my love for my family, my striving to build the Rising Cross Ranch, and my mission to free men from enslavement to the prejudices of other men.

I avoided being what others wanted or expected me to be. They had to take me for who and what I was, including my strengths and human frailties. I'd had to discern my way to choose the path that God laid before me. It was one of a million paths but narrower by virtue of my trust in Him. While the world manifested itself in chaos, I felt fully ordered. The more I grow, the greater man I become, the more I have to give. My survival depended upon the strength I'd built within myself.

With our goodbyes completed, we wound our way southward toward Bandera. We managed a good twenty-five miles and encountered no one. I did sense that we were being watched but figured it was either by friendly Indians or a party so small as to not want to take on our weapon arsenal.

We camped on the north bank of the first of our Medina River crossings. We felt confident enough to build a fire suitable for both cooking and warmth.

Hardy moved off into the woods near where we picketed our horses to keep first watch while Buck and I sat near the fire, drawing random designs in the soil with sticks.

"Is there ever a true winner in war, Jack?" This was a heavy question coming unexpectedly from my young brother. I was learning that his general quietness and tendency toward solitude hid a mind deeply considering questions about life.

"When Spirit Talker and I watched the Texas Rangers

attack the Comanche at the Battle of Little Robe Creek, the Indians were devastated in the surprise attack on the first encampment. The attack on the second Comanche encampment, the Quaqhadi Comanche, was nearly a stalemate. The Penateka Comanche in the third encampment was never attacked. Were the Comanche defeated? Had the Texas Rangers won? Captain Ford claimed success. The Comanche retreated."

"So, the Texas Rangers won?" Buck persisted.

"Seems like," I replied. I stirred the coals. "In the Noconi camp, children no longer had fathers, and some had no mothers. Brave warriors were killed. So, too, among the Quahadi. They would spend the next years as easy prey for marauding bands of other tribes. The Comanche that retreated did so with the pride of knowing they were ready for battle had they been attacked. Such were Buffalo Hump's *numunuu*. They rode out, ready to fight another day. Were they winners? I suggest they were not losers."

Buck chewed on that a bit. "War's a mess," he observed.

"It gets especially messy, when you look into an enemy's eyes and you have no alternative. You must kill or be killed. It grows a man up right fast, brother."

Hardy came running back to our campfire and began kicking dirt on it to snuff the flames. "Quiet!" he whispered.

I gave him an inquisitive look. My Sharps carbine was at hand, so I grabbed it and motioned to Buck to follow me. There was obviously some sort of danger to spark his actions.

"Whoever it be likely seen our fire," warned Hardy.

All was quiet. No horse hooves, no jingling of spurs or squeaking of leather. If somebody out there was approaching us in the dark, they were afoot. We moved away from where our campfire had been and crouched among some nearby trees.

"Help! Help!" came a chorus of cries. "Wolves!"

Zeb had made his presence known.

"Zeb!" I called. "You out there! Come in with hands high or I'll set them on you!" I commanded.

Zeb and his pack appeared, but ahead of them were three raggedly-uniformed Rebel soldiers. At least, I judged them by their butternut threads to be soldiers. I immediately suspected that they were deserters. Little did they know how lucky they were. A wolf's jaws are capable of serious damage. How Zeb managed to keep his pack from attacking the men was beyond my limited belief. It had to be a God thing.

The three men were unarmed and had no horses so far as we could tell. Thinking the worst, I reckoned they had planned to waylay us and steal our horses. Buck and Hardy kept their rifles leveled on them as they approached.

"Keep you hands high," I repeated. "Who are you and where are you from?" From what I could discern in the moonlight, they were a sad lot from their unshaven faces to torn Rebel uniforms and bare feet. I motioned to Buck to rekindle the fire.

They stood silently, surrounded by a pack of wolves and we three well-armed, tough-looking captors dressed in buckskins. All was quiet, as we sized each other up. Finally, one man spoke up and said, "I be Josh Turner. Me, Walt, and Billy here were among the troops that got routed at Glorieta Pass. Then, our supply train was burned. We joined with Captain Hunter, and some Apache named Mangas Coloradas put a whipping on us. We wasn't inclined to losing our hair so escaped the battle. Thought we was clear of trouble, when we lost our horses to some New Mexico cavalry led by a fellow named Carson. So, here we be."

Turner had said a mouthful. I thought back to our visit by Captain Pedigrew. Things apparently weren't going so well for the Confederacy west of Texas. The three must have run into the famed scout Kit Carson.

We were between a rock and a hard place. These were, in fact, deserters. To help them would put us at risk from Rebel units as being traitors. "Afraid we can't help y'all. I can share some coffee and a bit of grub, but then y'all must be on your way." Food and drink seemed the least I could do as a Christian.

The men breathed a collective sigh of relief, likely at not being shot. "Sorry to inflict ourselves upon you," apologized Turner.

Buck poured some coffee and distributed leftover venison.

"What were y'all up to before you enlisted?" I asked.

Walt answered first. "Worked the docks in Corpus. Everybody was enlisting, so I signed up."

"I farmed a place a few miles north of New Orleans," added Billy. "Got a wife an' three kids back there. Rebs came by and pressed me into service."

I looked at Turner.

"Can't say I was ever so accomplished as these two, sir."

"Really?"

"Punched beeves in California."

I gave Turner an incredulous look. I didn't take him for a cowboy, but then, a person could never be sure of such things. "How did you wind up with the Rebs?" It was a natural question.

"They were looking for someone who knew the trails

between California and Texas. It sounded like a great adventure at the time. They even promised me a ranch of my own. I fell for it." Turner's expression turned dour.

I shook my head at the trio's plight. Buck, Hardy, and I looked at each other. I think they knew what was coming. "Y'all know your lives aren't worth a hoot around here. If you're not shot, you'll be imprisoned."

The three deserters hung their heads hopelessly. By now, they'd sated their ravenous appetites but were at a loss as to what to do next.

"I might be able to help y'all out."

Buck and Hardy rolled their eyeballs, but not so the deserters could see.

"We're headed to Bandera on some business. If you men can stay here, we can bring back some boots and maybe a horse or two."

"You'd do that for us?" asked Turner.

"You must promise to head north to the North Platte Country near Fort Laramie. I have a friend there with a ranch, and he'll give you work on my say so." I enjoyed seeing their expressions lifted as hope entered their thinking. "Make no mistake, the trail is mighty danger-ous. Lots of Indians to contend with."

"How do we defend ourselves?"

I sighed. "We'll do what we can to help you there." I tried to sound reassuring. "We're heading out at sunrise. Y'all can consider my offer in the meantime." I glanced knowingly at Buck and Hardy. We'd have to be especially cautious despite the plausible stories the men offered. "I'll take next watch." Zeb and his pack faded into the nearby woods. I figured I could fall asleep, and my wolf friends would ensure our safety.

Hardy shook his head. His old Texas Ranger instincts gnawed at him, but he held his tongue.

———

WE LEFT the three deserters at the riverside camp and headed to Bandera. The day gave every hint at being a scorcher. As we headed down the trail, I turned to Hardy. "You don't approve?"

"Since yuh ask, you be right. Don't trust them a second."

"I understand. I hope I'm a decent judge of men. Well, we'll see if they're around on our way back from Bandera."

We didn't chat much the rest of the way to Bandera. The ride being mostly single file, it didn't exactly encourage conversation. We rode slowly into the town. There was nary a soul on the streets. We reined in at Klappenbach's store and dismounted.

I caught Stella's face in the window. She smiled when she saw me, then disappeared.

Moments later, Klappenbach himself burst through the front door. "Dang! You sure you're not a ghost, Jack O'Toole?" he exclaimed.

"Last time I checked, I was flesh and blood." I caught him in a bear hug, but we released quickly given the heat. "You've met Buck and Hardy here."

"What brings y'all to Bandera?" he said, as he ushered us into the store.

It was already hot and musty inside. Texas weather was living up to its reputation. When it was hot, it was searing hot. Cold would freeze your veins. We pulled up some chairs but quickly figured it was cooler to stand. I brought Klappenbach up to date as to goings on at Rising Cross Ranch. The conversation was going smoothly until I mentioned the three deserters and the fact that I intended to help them.

Klappenbach looked startled. "You three are luckier than you could possibly know. If you'd done some digging around, you'd have found their boots and guns. I suspect it was your wolf companion that kept them from their plan."

"What do you mean?" I couldn't help but ask.

Stella interrupted us with some coffee. There was nothing like hot liquid to make a hot day hotter, but she brewed great coffee.

Klappenbach continued. "Those three are spies for a nasty fellow out of Missouri named William Quantrill who is putting together a gang that might loosely be called cavalry. They're looking to make a mess of Union supply lines and killing as many folks as they can along the way. They're downright crafty and would have done y'all in if they'd had a chance. I expect they weren't quite figuring to run into trail smart men like you three."

Hardy was clearly holding back an "I told you so" look.

"I guarantee those three had weapons, uniforms, and horses stashed somewhere nearby. Probably be long gone, when y'all return to that spot."

I swallowed hard. So much for being a great judge of character. I thanked God for Zeb and his pack, as they undoubtedly spelled the difference between us being alive or dead. "Thanks, August." I took a long sip of coffee and felt a bead of sweat trickle down my back. "What's going on around Bandera these days?"

Now, Klappenbach chuckled. "Still got those dang-blasted camels up at Camp Verde. Rebs are using them to transport salt from San Antonio to Brownsville. Hear tell Rip Ford wants a bunch for patrolling the Rio Grande down around Fort Brown. Other than that, Bandera's been quiet. Apache stay clear, and there have been no

Mexican troublemakers this far north, though that Juarez fellow has been stirring things up down there. Word has it, the insane French Emperor Napolean is of a mind to step in." He paused. "Trade has slowed quite a bit thanks to the Yankee blockade on the Gulf and fewer cattle drives."

"Looks like the fighting's going to continue for a while," I observed. "Reckon the Yankees will outlast the Rebs."

Klappenbach stroked his chin thoughtfully. "I hear tell that General Lee, the one that used to patrol here in Texas, is leading the Confederate army in the east. He's apparently winning more than losing, more than I can say for Rebel forces around Missouri and Louisiana. New Orleans just fell to the Union. Lee's hankering to take the fighting north."

I shrugged. "All we've seen were a troop of foragers and the three ne'er-do-wells we met on the trail down here. A small war party of young Noconi Comanche gave us a tussle at Rising Cross, but we dissuaded them right quick. With so many menfolk off fighting, the Indians have gotten overconfident. Guess we've been lucky."

"You fixing to get another cattle drive going?"

I nodded. "We have a lot of fat beeves. Better to drive them north."

Klappenbach smiled. "Can't blame you for avoiding the Confederate script. It's going to become worthless as the war lingers on."

Hardy chimed in with a chuckle and a knowing look. "Sold a dozen nags to Rebel foragers for script."

"Anything we can do for you, Jack?" asked Klappenbach.

"I just had a hankering to ride down this way and be sure y'all were okay, August." I looked over at Buck and

Hardy. "Of course, I had to bring an escort. Skillful as my woodsman skills are, we don't travel alone these days."

We dined with August and Stella, figuring to head for home in the morning. I was curious as to what we might find, when we arrived at the place where we'd encountered the Quantrill spies. We were being educated on the chaos of what many called a civil war.

TWELVE
DUPLICITY

WE BADE the Klappenbach farewell and rode out of Bandera in the morning. We did manage to stuff our saddlebags with some notions. Mine included a new dress for Blue Flower, some sewing thread and needles, a little frock for Nadua, and toys for Isa, George, and Peter.

But there was more. We passed a ramshackle clapboard house on the way out of town, and a young man in a Rebel tunic was sitting on the front stairs with a bandage over one eye and a missing arm. He gave us an unforgettably mournful look from his good eye as we passed. I wondered how many more of his ilk would pay a steep price for the supposed glory of the South. I respectfully tapped my fingers to the brim of my hat as we passed on by.

We took the same route we'd used on the journey southward, so by late afternoon we reached the spot where we'd encountered the three Rebels. As Klappenbach had predicted, they were gone. It was in my nature to investigate, so I got Shorty and Buck to join me in carefully searching the area from which they'd been driven out by Zeb's pack. Sure enough, among wolf paw prints were those of shod horses. The duplicity of the trio was confirmed.

"The good Lord was sure lookin' out fer us," said Hardy.

I agreed. "Something still doesn't feel right about those three. My bones are telling me we haven't seen the last of them."

"What else are your bones telling you, dear brother?" asked Buck.

"We'd better be extra cautious from here on." I looked off into the woods and saw Zeb waiting for us to resume our journey.

"I'm with yuh there, boss. I be aimin' to keep my hair an' stay above the snakes." Hardy chuckled at his humor as he spurred his horse and headed up the trail with us falling in behind him.

———

IT FINALLY OCCURRED to me that Quantrill's men had to be up to more than waylaying the likes of me, Buck, and Hardy. What could it be? While Central Texas had never been a hotbed of abolitionists, there was general support for the Confederacy. Most of the men caught up in prewar emotions that led to vigilante behaviors and minor skirmishes had enlisted and gone off to find the glories of battle. Thinking back to the wounded man we'd passed in Bandera, I reckoned they'd be disappointed as concerned glory.

I fell back, as that old intuition told me to be watching our back trail. I looked over to my left, and Zeb must have been sensing the same thing. Nevertheless, and despite my growing concern, I let my trail mates get perhaps a quarter mile ahead of me.

We hadn't ridden but another mile, and I was sore and tempted to call out to Hardy and Buck to fall back, when there was a ruckus ahead of me. Two rifle shots were fired into the air, and the jangle of sabers carried in the crisp midday air.

I turned Big Red toward Zeb and headed off the trail. I heard shouts, but wasn't fully able to make out what was being said. Clearly, Buck and Hardy had run into trouble. The big question was what sort of enemy I was facing.

I slid from Big Red's saddle and grabbed my bow and arrows. I hefted the bow. I'd made it myself following instructions from Spirit Talker, my Comanche brother. I'd fashioned it from juniper and tipped its ends with buffalo horn. It was short but surprisingly powerful. I'd hit a target at two hundred yards and used it to drive an arrow clean through a deer at a hundred feet. I'd feathered my arrows with buzzard wing quills and made arrowheads chipped to razor-sharp perfection from flint. I gave a thought to poisoning the arrowheads by running them through cattle dung, but demurred. I gave a brief thought to the Sharps carbine, but decided this was a job for the silent effectiveness of the arrow. Whoever had attacked Buck and Hardy had best be ready for a nasty fight.

I made my way through the woods and thick undergrowth as quickly as possible. Zeb trailed with me as though knowing not to get ahead of me. Perhaps he sensed that charging armed men might not end well. We soon reached a place where the forest formed a natural divide around a large boulder. I paused to pray for success in rescuing Buck and Hardy, then climbed to the top to get a view of what lay ahead. This is where my decision to wear moccasins rather than boots had been a good idea.

I crawled across the top of the boulder. Not more than fifty feet away, the three Rebels, supposedly with Quantrill, were grilling my brother and my foreman as to where I was. The man who'd called himself Josh Turner held the tip of his saber to Hardy's chest.

The three captors looked nothing like the trio of derelicts we'd encountered a couple of nights back. They were decked out in fancy cavalry uniforms with brass buttons, gold lace filigree, hats with gold braid, and polished black boots. The man called Turner had stripes on his sleeve, so I judged him to be a sergeant. Their horses stood nearby and were as fine a horseflesh as might be found.

I signaled Zeb to stay. My experience told me that if I eliminated the leader, his men would likely panic. These men could have stronger constitutions, but I doubted it. The idea of killing another human was detestable to me, but these men gave me no choice. They were threatening those close to me. I was sure God would forgive me.

Taking a deep breath, I raised to one knee, nocked an arrow to my bowstring, pulled it back, aimed, and let fly. At this distance, the arrow nearly passed clean through Turner's body. The saber instantly dropped from his hand with a clatter on the rocks, as he looked down at the feathered end of my arrow protruding from his chest. Turner dropped to his knees then fell forward on his face. His companions were aghast. Just as they were about to gather their wits, Zeb leaped into the fray. Buck and Hardy quickly saw the opportunity. While Zeb held a firm bloody grip on one man's leg, Buck and Hardy wrestled the other to the ground and trussed him with his own belt.

I have no idea what made me do it, but I stood with arms and legs akimbo, held my bow aloft, beat my chest with my free hand, and sent a triumphant wolf howl to the skies. It was apparently wolfish enough to make Zeb release his grip. No matter that, Buck and Hardy were already tying the man's hands and checking out the wound in his leg. I calmly climbed down from the rock.

I strode easy-like over to the scene of the brief but decidedly violent battle. Buck's and Hardy's expressions revealed the great relief they felt at my timely rescue. "Y'all okay?" I asked. They shook their heads vigorously as they stood with their prisoners. The man named Josh Turner was deader than a doornail. It may sound gross, but I bent over him and managed with a strong pull to retrieve my arrow as it had nearly penetrated completely through man. Good arrows were not easy to make, and there was no point in wasting this one.

"Hardy, gather their weapons and horses." I turned my attention to our prisoners while Hardy made sure all was secure. "Which one of you is Walt and which is Billy?"

They were silent.

"Humph! Tongues tied?"

Hardy picked up on where I was headed. "Not agin', boss?"

"Shucks, if they aren't going to use their tongues, might as well cut them out," I deadpanned as I pulled out my Bowie knife. "Bowie knife makes it cleaner than those Comanche knives."

The sheer horror written across the prisoners' faces was worth the threat. Tongues started wagging. "N-n-no...I'm Billy."

I waved my knife. "Guess you're Walt." I pointed the knife his way.

Walt nodded nervously.

"It's good to be able to put names on their tombstones," I said with a hint of venom in my tone.

"We going to hang 'em or shoot 'em, boss?"

I scratched my chin thoughtfully. "Let's see what they have to say. We could always feed them to Zeb and his pack."

"What if they lie?" asked Buck. He was beginning to get into the very real game I was playing.

"Ever hear of death by a thousand cuts?" I teased. "Every lie earns a cut." With that, I turned to the one called Billy. "I hear tell that y'all ride with a fellow named William Quantrill. That true?"

Billy nodded nervously.

"Did you hear anything, Hardy?" I taunted and stepped toward him with my knife.

"Y-y-yes. We be on our way to Missouri to join Quantrill."

"Why the disguises and why attack us?"

"Thet were Turner's idee," retorted Walt. "Kin y'all bandage my leg?"

I had to admit his leg was bleeding a bit. "Buck, please fetch Big Red. There are bandages in my saddlebag." I turned back to Billy. "I'm thinking Quantrill must be desperate to recruit the likes of y'all. I'm asking once more. Why did you attack us?"

"Josh said it be practice," admitted Billy.

"And today?" I pressed.

"Josh, he weren't none too happy 'bout the other night. Reckoned to ambush y'all."

I shook my head. "Dang, Hardy. These men seem to keep telling the truth. They're not giving me a chance to cut on them."

"What we gonna do with 'em, boss?" Hardy raised a question of serious concern.

Buck showed up with Big Red and pulled some bandage material from my saddlebag.

"You gonna waste bandages?" asked Hardy.

"We can't be letting a man, even one so unworthy, bleed out. But I do have an idea to teach these men a lesson."

Buck went to work bandaging Walt's leg.

"Untie them and grab a shovel, Hardy." By now I'd retrieved my Sharps carbine. "Y'all are going to bury your friend here. Start digging."

They took turns digging deep enough in the rocky soil to bury Turner.

With the burial completed, Billy and Walt were now standing before us with my Sharps aimed in their direction. "Take off your boots," I directed.

The men, incentivized by the Sharps carbine pointed at them, complied quickly.

"Now, remove your pants."

They exchanged tentative glances at each other but removed their trousers as I demanded.

"Shirts," I directed.

The two were now standing before us in naught but their underwear.

"Start walking," I commanded them, pointing them westward. I didn't want them heading to Bandera or coming anywhere near Rising Cross Ranch to the north. If they were lucky, they'd avoid Indians.

"Wh-what?! Yuh can't be doin' this," pleaded Walt.

I fired the Sharps, aiming just inches from Walt's wounded leg. "You deaf? I said start walking. You're lucky to get away with your lives."

The two looked longingly at the pile of their clothes

and their horses. With sighs and shaking of heads, they began reluctantly limping their way down the rough trail yelping at each rock stepped upon.

I looked over at Buck and Walt. "Looks as though we have three fine horses to add to our herd," I said, nonplussed.

Buck shook his head. "You're amazing, brother."

What could I do? I shrugged, smiled, and pointed to Heaven. I ran my fingers through Zeb's mane and mounted up. "Let's go home."

———

WE RODE CAUTIOUSLY ONWARD. The string of horses and the goodies we'd purchased made us a potential target of Indian raiders with grudges against the White man and of evil folks that looked to steal rather than earn an honest living.

I gave serious thought to riding through the night, but thick clouds were blotting the moon and stars, thus making the trail treacherous. At about fifteen miles from home and with the sun casting its pinkish-orange glow across the western horizon, we found a place to cold camp. An overhanging rock afforded cover, and there was plenty of grass for the horses.

I placed my saddle against the trunk of a live oak growing from beside the rock.

"How do you decide, brother?" This journey to Bandera had inspired Buck to ask me questions that had apparently been lingering on his mind.

I glanced over at him questioningly. "Decide what?"

"How to treat those with evil on their minds," he explained.

I had never really thought about it. My actions were

second nature to me as though inbred. "I guess it was the Bible teaching Pa gave us, Buck. I learned that God taught us to be positive in our lives, to be joyful, to look at the upsides of things, and especially strive to be forgiving and merciful. From my Comanche brother Spirit Talker, I learned both confidence in my strengths as supported by my faith as well as contentment but to always be on guard so they're never taken away. I learned that evil folks tended to be bitter, hostile, and wicked-minded. Over time, I learned to discern these traits in folks." I had learned that evil folks are often so filled with sin that you cannot get inside their minds to find any lurking goodness.

"But?" pressed Buck.

"As to deciding, I earnestly strive to avoid killing. I have killed animals to both eat and protect myself. As to humans, it's a lot tougher because humans can experience guilt, remorse, and shame over evil deeds. Discernment is an acquired skill. It means looking as deeply as possible into an evildoer's soul. Can they be redeemed? What drove them to break the laws of God and man? Then, what's an appropriate response." I paused and looked off at the moonlight trying to break through the clouds. "I've made mistakes, Buck. They've nearly been the death of me. But, some, like Brawny Jones, turned from their sinful ways. Deciding? It's a learned skill, brother, and we can only hope to survive the teaching of it. It's important to not overreact to circumstances. Bad things often happen when you permit the emotions of the moment to rule your head."

Buck nodded, lay his head against his saddle, and fell asleep.

"I'll take first watch," I whispered to Hardy. As I climbed to the top of the rock with my rifle, I thought on what I'd shared with Buck. There were many lost souls in our world. I had learned that my happiness depended on a faith that led me to strive to be positive and enthusiastic about life, to be ever optimistic, and to aim to be as forgiving and merciful as possible. Thanks mostly to Pa's teachings from the Bible, I found myself motivated to enjoy and build upon God's bounty. It left me with a core of peace, tranquility, and satisfaction that others might mistake for indifference but was, in fact, part of what Spirit Talker called me strong *sunipu*. Lord knows, I'd fought bears, mountain lions, rattlesnakes, and all sorts of hostile humans. It was the depth of my God-given character that drove me to help the Comanche and to fight against slavery. I sat there on that rock, listening to the sounds of the night. Coyotes howled, crickets chirped, and Hardy snored.

THIRTEEN
CATTLE DRIVE?

TO MANY FOLKS, it may have been counterintuitive for a Texas cattleman to drive a herd of longhorns north in the midst of a war. Ranching is a business, and I much preferred being paid in gold rather than Confederate script. Most of Texas had been spared the horrors of war, as action tended to concentrate along the coast. Being located better than a day's ride west of Austin, we weren't convenient to foragers looking to feed the Rebel army. That was surely a blessing, though we still had to survive and that meant bringing in the income needed to purchase supplies.

Sam Collins contributed a couple of hundred head from his Circle C, so we assembled a lusty herd of better than eight hundred longhorns and reckoned to drive them to George Freeman's place up on the North Platte River.

The Great Western Trail had been discovered by now, though drovers had moved the trail about a hundred miles east from the couple of drives we'd already put together. The present Great Western Trail tended to be a tad easier than the trail we'd broken, though I feared that the openness of the landscape offered less cover from marauding Indians.

"Must you go?" asked Blue Flower. She gave me that look, the one that had pulled me in years ago with some sort of irresistible power.

I'd thought long and hard on whether I should stay at Rising Cross or head up the drive with Shorty as trail master. My loving wife and I had discussed it, but she remained concerned as to the safety of our family here in Texas so long as hostilities lingered on. I asked myself whether I was letting my pridefulness in heading up another trail drive get in the way of making a more prudent decision? Was I basking overmuch in my successes in surviving the war thus far? Had it gone to my head?

My ever-wise wife, gifted in the ways of her Comanche ancestors, must have been thinking the same thing. I'd given her a book of poetry at Christmas, and she now thrust it before me. It was open to a poem by a fellow named Percy Bysshe Shelley. I thought it a funny name but dared not laugh. I began to read the poem to myself.

Blue Flower interrupted. "Speak words," she insisted. This was smart. The spoken word does tend to have greater impact.

I read aloud,

"I met a traveler from an antique land
Who said: Two vast and trunkless legs of stone
Stand in the desert. Near them, on the sand,
Half sunk, a shattered visage lies, whose frown,
And wrinkled lip, and sneer of cold command,
Tell that its sculptor well those passions read
Which yet survive, stamped on these lifeless things,

The hand that mocked them, and the heart that fed.
And on the pedestal these words appear:
'My name is Ozymandias, king of kings:
Look on my works ye mighty and despair!'
Nothing beside remains. Round the decay
Of that colossal wreck, boundless and bare
The lone and level sands stretch far away."

I LOOKED DEEPLY into Blue Flower's eyes. *My dear God,* I thought. So beautiful, so danged perceptive.

The expression crossing her face oozed compassion for my ego, for my pride in building Rising Cross, and my mission to fight slavery, but her words cut my pride off at its knees.

"Nothing beside remains." Blue Flower repeated Shelley's words.

My duty was here at Rising Cross with my family. It was the truly prideful action that I must take. I laid a knowing look upon her. "Shorty can head the drive. I'll stay here," I stated firmly.

Blue Flower buried herself in me. She hugged so hard that I thought she might squeeze the very life from me. The poetry book fell to the floor and well...

———

I WATCHED A BIT LONGINGLY, as Shorty headed the herd out with nine drovers and Perez pulling up the rear with his wagon. Sam Collins had lent two drovers to the drive and we'd managed to lure a couple of cowpokes from a neighboring ranch who were experienced and too old to have joined the Rebel cause. It was mid-June, and with any luck, they'd all be back by sometime in early October.

I'd given Shorty a packet of a half dozen of my letters about slavery and surviving the war in the Confederacy for George to pass on to the newspapers. I had no idea as to whether the *New York Tribune* received my letters, much less published any.

I took stock of our situation. There was now me and Blue Flower with our four children, Will and my sister Kate and their two little ones, and Isaac and Sarah up the lane with their family. Among us, we'd run the ranch with hope that we'd not face threats from Rebels or Indians. With most of our beeves headed north, the remaining livestock were manageable. Among Will, Isaac, and me, we still never ventured out alone. We made sure that our wives practiced their marksmanship, as we could never be certain from whence trouble might come, and we'd likely need every gun to defend ourselves.

As the dust from the herd faded into the distance, I looked down at Isa and George standing beside me and mimicking my longing look at the disappearing cattle. The twins were nearly six years old and would soon be out from under Blue Flower's tutelage. We had committed ourselves to the Comanche way of educating children until they were ten or so years old at which time they'd be turned over to the men for training in the skills of survival—to hunt and to fight. It wouldn't be long until they were fully under my wings. I hoped this war would be a matter of history by the time they were of age.

———

I RECALL that it was early on a Tuesday morning that I emerged from the barn and came face-to-face with what first struck me as an incredibly frightful apparition. A fearsome rider sat a pinto pony decked in war paint. Broad black warpaint crossed the rider's grim face, half hidden behind a buffalo-skin shield and brandishing a war lance decorated with eagle feathers. My jaw dropped until I spotted the telltale scars across the painted face and the eyes that meant no harm to Pohya Isa.

"Mukwooru!" I declared.

The mighty warrior slipped from his saddle and bounded into a brotherly embrace. "Pohya Isa *pabi*," he exclaimed.

"*Hoikwa? Kwakuru?*" I asked reflexively. Was he hunting or fighting? From the warpaint, I'd guess the latter. Then, I recalled my manners. "*Ana o'a hi'it?*" I invited Spirit Talker to eat with us.

Spirit Talker stood before me with his hands on my shoulders and looked into my eyes. "Much war. Mukwooru strong *sunipu*. Pray much. Fight Kiowa... Apache...Comanche *tabu*."

"*Tabu*," I repeated. Cowards indeed to feast on mostly defenseless homesteads and small towns while war raged to the east.

Ten Penateka Comanche warriors rode up behind Spirit Talker. They were every inch as formidable-looking as he. I was now gazing on a collection of decorated shields, war lances, bows and arrows, war clubs, a handful of assorted rifles, and plenty of warpaint.

Blue Flower appeared in the doorway to our home. "Mukwooru *kamakuna!*" she cried out and ran toward Spirit Talker.

Warrior mouths collectively dropped, as they recognized the daughter of Buffalo Hump. Imagine, if you will, a fully-outfitted Comanche warrior embracing his petite sister in front of the warriors he led.

"*Ana o'a hi'it?*" Blue Flower repeated my invitation and motioned all the band to join us.

To put it mildly, it was a wonderful relief to have Spirit Talker with us, if only briefly. The band dismounted and sat on the gallery, while Blue Flower whipped up some Comanche-worthy grub.

"*Hoikwa* Utes," noted Spirit Talker. "Two-day north. *Kuuna tosa* house."

Spirit Talker and his band were acting like a prairie police force. Apparently, some Utes had burned down the home of some White folk, and my Comanche brother was intent on teaching the hostiles a lesson.

Blue Flower set a table under the rook to the gallery and laid out all manner of delicious morsels, including a stack of fresh-baked bear sign.

But here I pause. It was obvious where Spirit Talker's heart was in protecting me and my fellow settlers on what had been the lands upon which they alone had lived. What he did gave me hope for the future.

Spirit Talker raised his hands to the sky. "Praise Taa Narumi for food. Thank Christ. Amen." It was short and impactful. He'd not forgotten what I'd taught and what he'd clearly taken to heart. Most notably, his warriors joined in his blessing.

The Comanche dug into Blue Flower's spread of bacon, eggs, and biscuits. When the bear sign was all-too-quickly devoured, The warriors looked pleadingly from Spirit Talker to me. I half-feared the band would rebel if not fed more of the treats, but Blue Flower had anticipated this and baked more. Honestly, I was absolutely amazed that she did so much in so little time. Maybe, it was a little of

Perez's influence from feeding groups of drovers on the cattle drives.

"Mukwooru come back soon," shared Spirit Talker, as he wiped the last traces of bear sign from his chin. "*Hoikwa* Utes," he reminded his warriors and nodded toward their ponies.

The fearsome-looking warriors headed toward their horses without hesitation, each thanking Blue Flower in an almost-reverent manner. Once mounted, they acknowledged me by joining their hands across their chests as signs of peace. I felt blessed to have had such influence on these Comanche simply through my enduring faith in God. Spirit Talker and I had long before bonded in trust, love, faith, and hope for the future.

"Go with Taa Narumi," I said to the warriors. "Go with God." I guess I had delivered in a fashion not unlike what I'd heard of Saint Patrick in Ireland, whereby he'd taken the better parts of the pagan culture and incorporated them into the Christian faith so as to convert them to God's church. I watched with my arm around Blue Flower, as the warriors departed to hunt the Utes.

————

THE SUMMER FLEW BY. We heard tidbits of the war's happenings. A Rebel general named Longstreet had routed a Yankee army at the Second Battle of Bull Run, Harpers Ferry had fallen to a fellow named Stonewall Jackson, but the Union troops had put a serious licking on the Confederate army at Antietam. It was in this context that Shorty, Hardy, Buck, and the couple of drovers who'd decided to return showed up one late September afternoon. They were dirty as can be and decidedly trail-weary. Importantly, they'd returned unscathed. Perez and the trail drive wagon were yet to come into view.

I wanted to throw buckets of fresh water on them before welcoming hugs, but embraced them anyway. "Welcome home!" I exclaimed.

Shorty gave me a somewhat rueful look. "Might not be so happy, boss, when yuh see what's comin' behind us." He nodded over his shoulder at the dust cloud kicking up behind them.

I looked out toward the west pasture and found myself cursing under my breath while asking God's forgiveness simultaneously. "Y'all ready?" I asked Shorty.

He nodded. "Locked an' loaded, boss."

"Head inside and man the ports," I ordered. Zeb appeared as if from nowhere and sat beside me, his eyes focused on the threat before us. Blue Flower snuck up behind me and placed the shotgun in my hands. I hid it behind my legs.

Soon enough, Rowdy Sikes and about two dozen butternut-clad riders came galloping into our yard and reined in hard.

Sikes and I eyeballed each other. I sensed that I faced a man pretty much unhindered by scruples. "What brings you to Rising Cross Ranch, Mr. Sikes?" I demanded.

"It's Captain Sikes to you, O'Toole," declared Sikes. The former vigilante now had a commission to legitimize his violent inclinations.

It didn't matter whether the officer's commission was earned or bought, the man posed an immediate threat. He wouldn't show here except to cause trouble. "What's your business, Captain?" I asked with special emphasis on his rank. I might have sounded just a tad derisive.

"How come you ain't enlisted, O'Toole?" challenged

Sikes. He finally took the time to look beyond me to my house and couldn't miss the arsenal of Sharps carbine muzzles poking from the gun ports of each window. "You sonof…"

He paused, as I brought my shotgun up from behind me. "If you need to feed your troops, captain, I'd be obliged. If you're looking for trouble, you'll be the first to die." I rightly reckoned that Sikes was basically a coward and would back down against any display of strength.

He looked at Zeb but dared not lock eyes. It was clear that he was sizing us up. Sikes snorted. "At ease!" he called to his men. "You win, O'Toole…this time." He said the last two words mostly out of earshot of his troops. He dismounted with a jangle of saber and considerable creaking of leather. He stood before me with hands raised in a supplicating gesture. "I don't aim to do no harm, O'Toole. Yuh can lower the scattergun."

I gave him my best squinty-eyed, suspicious look and lowered the shotgun muzzle. I felt secure with the knowledge that a half dozen rifles backed me up. "You seen any fighting, captain?"

Sikes nodded. "Got whupped at Galveston a few months back," he admitted. "Didn't let us in the danged fight."

So, his answer was that he had yet to bloody his sword. "What brings you here, Captain?"

Sikes went to his saddlebag and pulled out a newspaper which he proceeded to unfold as he walked over to me. "You know who this is, O'Toole? I expect you travel with these sorts of folks." He displayed the front page and pointed to a small headline. "Who is Zebediah Smith?" he asked.

The headline read *Rancher Resists Rebels* and what followed was one of my letters. I shrugged. I'd ask the

Lord later to forgive my lying. "I haven't a clue who might have written that, captain. Shoot, it's most likely fiction. Who'd dare write that?"

Sikes knew full well that I'd be one to dare such a deed. "We ran into a fella west of here name of Cutter Kincaid. He said he knew nothin'. Same fer some frens of yers back in Fredericksburg."

I gulped. Had they done something to my old friend Kincaid? To the McGregors? Reggie? "Why don't y'all find some Yankees to fight, Captain Sikes?"

He laid a suspicious glare on me. "Yuh better not know anything 'bout this Smith fella, O'Toole," he threatened.

"And what might you try to do about it?" I challenged him.

He glanced down at my shotgun, noted the hammers both pulled back, and then at the muzzles poking from the gun ports like porcupine quills. "Mebbe another day," he growled.

"You'd best be on your way, Captain, unless you become of a peaceful mind. We can deliver fine Texas hospitality in either lead or meat." I could see that Sikes was searching for a way to save face in front of his troops. I smiled. I had won this battle. "Y'all care for some coffee, maybe some bear sign?" I saw that the troops heard my mention of the sweet baked treats. I knew Blue Flower had baked some that very morning. There weren't two dozen, but she could make more.

Sikes visibly relaxed. "We'd be much obliged, Mr. O'Toole," he said respectfully.

Blue Flower had been listening from the house and emerged with a platter filled with bear sign.

I could see that Sikes was put off at my having married a Comanche, but he held his tongue.

The troops held no such prejudices in the face of delicious treats.

By now, my sister Kate had brewed fresh coffee and filled as many trooper cups as she could before heading back to brew more.

With bellies satisfied and having imbibed coffee better than any they could hope to brew on the trail, I don't think Sikes could have inspired his men to battle us even were we to wave an abolitionist banner from the rooftop. Sikes ordered saddles and prepared to head his men out. I truly think he didn't quite know what to make of me. Perhaps—just perhaps, mind you—I was having a good impact on him. It was clear that he carried some sort of demons inside, but my strength, combined with gracious hospitality, befuddled him enough to question whatever evils lurked under his skin. "Much obliged for your hospitality, Mr. O'Toole," he said with a heartfelt tone. Sikes saluted smartly.

"Y'all are welcome back any time, Captain." I truly hoped that I might have an opportunity to fully turn Sikes's heart.

Shorty and the others came from the house one by one to watch the Rebels depart. "Doggone, boss. You and Blue Flower be downright amazin'," he said with a look of utter astonishment.

I winked at Buck per our conversation back on the trail coming home from Bandera. "It's God's work, Shorty."

FOURTEEN
WAR ENDS

I STOOD on the gallery savoring a freshly brewed coffee while scanning the horizon and simultaneously listening to Isa, George, and Peter play the games that little boys play. I laughed inwardly as they took sides as Indians versus Whites. They didn't yet appreciate that the blood of both races ran in their veins.

Blue Flower joined me with three-year-old Nadua in her arms. "Think war end?" she asked.

I nodded. "Could be," I offered hopefully. It was late April 1865, and it seemed that the war might never end. During my travels around our spread over the past couple of months, I had twice seen columns of defeated-looking butternut-clad soldiers heading away from where battles had raged. President Lincoln issued his Emancipation Proclamation in January 1863. The news had reached us mid-year about the Rebel debacle at Gettysburg not far from where I'd spent the first fourteen years of my life. I reckoned that it was the beginning of the end for the Confederacy. The South had taken a solid whipping at Vicksburg, some Union General named Grant was scoring victory after victory, and a General Sherman took Atlanta and engineered a devastating scorched-earth march to the sea. Battles had been won and lost by both sides, but the Rebels were getting the worst of the war as supply lines were destroyed and enthusiasm weakened. I sighed. We had dodged any interaction with the war. I chalked that up to our remote location. "I reckon I ought to partner with Buck and check out the north range," I said with a smile at Blue Flower.

She nodded and handed Nadue to me.

The little bundle was worthy of her name, *keep warm with us*, as she snuggled against my shoulder and pulled playfully at my ear. A play arrow clattered across the wooden boards of the gallery. "The boys are itching for grown-up action," I said with a sigh. Their growing up was happening far too quickly.

As we were about to head inside, the sound of a galloping horse caught our attention. We paused as horse and rider came to a skidding stop in a cloud of dust.

"Lee surrendered!" he announced and was about to charge on.

The rider was about to gallop off when I called out. "Stop! You've about baked that horse. Ride any more like that and you're going to kill it for sure." Indeed, lather and trail dust were thickly pasted all over the front of the horse. The poor beast's breathing was labored. "I'll trade you horses, but you can't be riding like that." I figured I might save the cayuse from an all-too-certain fate.

The rider gave me a baleful sort of look but slid from his saddle. He sure was all-fired excited about getting the word out. Could hardly blame him. His news was a relief to most folks.

"Will!" I called. "Please fetch one of those mustangs and swap out the tack." By my calculation, the rider would push his mount again, but a mustang was a heartier breed and might even bite his rider if pushed too hard. I'd have traded a mule, if I had one. I turned to the rider. "This won't take long. Where did this Lee surrender?"

He looked at me through excitement-glazed eyes. "Place called Appomattox. General Lee surrendered to General Grant. Sad day for the South." He began to calm a bit.

I had to agree that it was a sad day for the South, as had been the days filling the preceding years of war. "You do any fighting?" I was trying to delay the man while Will swapped out the tack.

The young man raised his head with a prideful air. "I got nicked by a minie ball at Gettysburg." He showed me an ugly scar on his forearm. "Lucky it didn't blow my arm off," he added.

"Well, thanks for your sacrifice," I commented. By now, he was breathing easier. "WE appreciate you spreading the news, but caution you to keep your horse under you. You won't get far on foot."

By this time, Will strolled up, leading the mustang.

The grateful rider was soon heading off, albeit at a canter rather than gallop—at least until he was out of our sight.

I stood a moment with hands on hips. The war was over. Now what? We had roughly five hundred head grazing our range. A trail drive was a possibility. I was about to head to the barn to saddle up Big Red, when Hank Johnson came riding in. Johnson was Sam Collins's foreman at the Circle C. His sad expression surprised me in the wake of the rider who'd left but moments before.

"What's up, Hank?" I ventured.

He slowly dismounted. It was then that I realized he'd been crying. "Lincoln..." he muttered. "He bin kilt."

"What?!"

Johnson locked eyes with me. "Some two-bit actor name of Wilkes Boothe shot him in the back of his head."

The world had just turned upside down. Lee had surrendered, and days later, traitors assassinated Abraham Lincoln. I turned to Will. "Gather the hands and family, Will."

Will had heard Johnson and went off, shaking his head sadly. Soon, everyone except Buck and Hardy who were out on the range, had gathered at the big house.

Blue Flower looked curiously at me, wondering what I was about to impart.

They couldn't miss Johnson standing beside me with a sad expression etched across his prairie-toughened face.

"Hank here brought news that President Lincoln has been killed by an assassin." I let that sink in. "I expect there will be a lot of resentment against the South. Our loyalty to the Union may be tested." I knew that owners of plantations captured by the Union army had been required to take a loyalty oath and their assets— including slaves—seized. The slaves were supposed to be paid ten dollars a month to work in the fields.

The faces looking back at me were in collective shock at the news. I couldn't begin to imagine what hopes and fears swirled within the minds of these family and ranch hands. Despite our collective faith in God's protection, it was mostly fear that took top billing in this theater.

"Andrew Johnson will be president. I have no idea what to expect, but I hear he's no Abraham Lincoln."

"What are we to do, boss?" asked Hardy.

"Let's give it a few days. We shouldn't make any rash decisions," I counseled. I feared we'd be facing ugly reactions to how the end of the war would be handled. I thought back to words my pa had read to me from the Bible. I think it was from Romans about evil men's throats being as open graves with deception on their tongues and snake venom under their lips. There would be bitterness and ongoing bloodshed. Peace would yet be a long time coming. It would take all of our strength to withstand hate-filled days yet to come. Many Rebels would not fully shed their uniforms. Some were undoubtedly brave men, but many, not so. In my brief life experience across the frontier, I observed that truly brave men quaked with fear at the prospect of battle. Despite my faith, I'd certainly felt fearful in the face of danger be it from bears, mountain lions, or Indians. In fact, I reckoned that the brave man who knows no fear is an irrational being likely to blunder to a fool's death. It seemed to be about courage and cowardice, and I sure never featured myself a coward.

Blue Flower tapped my arm. "What Jack think?"

I was being called Jack, not my Comanche-earned name, Pohya Isa. I was not *walking with any wolves* at this moment. I gazed out at the gathering, then looked off at the distant horizon and the wispy clouds above. "Y'all go about your tasks. We'll gather to talk about this in a few days." There was no immediacy. I surely needed to think on it myself. I feared that Texas might become a veritable cauldron of vengeful post-war action.

"Give my best to Sam," I advised Johnson, as he mounted up to return to the Circle C.

Blue Flower gently grasped my elbow, led me inside our house, and motioned me to sit. She poured coffee and joined me at the kitchen table. The boys were quiet as though sensing the seriousness of the moment. "Much danger," she observed.

I nodded. I dared not overreact. "Yes." If she expected more, it would not, could not come. "We wait." It wasn't a reassuring answer, but we had to know more in order to make the big decisions that lay ahead.

A mere two weeks later, we learned that my old friend Rip Ford had soundly defeated Union troops at a place called Palmito Ranch near Brownsville. Next day, he learned of Lee's surrender, reluctantly released all the Union prisoners, and retreated. It would be the very last formal battle of the war.

———

THE CONFEDERACY HAD BEEN DEFEATED. It didn't take long for what was called reconstruction to take hold. The US Army arrived to take possession of the state, restore order, and enforce emancipation. I heard that it was a nasty business most everywhere throughout the South but especially here in Texas. A set of laws called the Texas Black Code were put into place to facilitate the readmission of states into the Union. There were huge numbers of freed slaves with nowhere to go and no way to make a livelihood. A short-lived attempt by General Sheridan to offer former slaves reparations of forty acres and a mule on lands near Charleston, South Carolina, was reversed by President Johnson who returned the land to its previous owners. This reconstruction business hit Texas hard.

Johnson appointed Union General Andrew Hamilton as provisional governor and he granted amnesty to ex-rebels who promised to support the Union. A Freedmen's Bureau was established, and significant political and social changes exercised. A new state constitution was introduced but failed to pass muster with the Federals, and the formerly all-powerful plantation owners struggled with breakouts of racial violence and attempts to establish segregationist laws. The Texas Rangers were disbanded and replaced by a state police force comprised of many former slaves. Freed slaves were subject to all sorts of abused, including beatings and shootings. Along the Texas coastal corridor, many Blacks were still held in bondage, though I heard that the most outrageous deeds were committed by outlaws and renegade Indians up in the northernmost reaches of Texas.

———

THE MORNING GREETED us with heat and humidity. It was so hot that my sweat was sweating. Any dust kicked up by what little breeze wafted across the range instantly stuck to my body. I was standing there with Buck and Hardy and wiping my brow with an already sopping-wet bandana, when we heard horses and a wagon of some sort approaching.

It hadn't taken long to be visited by officials seeking to exercise what power they could muster over ranch operations at Rising Cross. The facts that we'd never owned slaves and I'd run an underground railroad of sorts, mattered not.

They pulled up in a fancy coach with an armed escort mounted on some sorry-looking nags. The uniformed escort was a mix of Whites, Blacks, and a Mexican. They apparently were part of the newly formed state police force. They sported Henry rifles displayed across their laps. Two passengers dressed in what at one time were likely the very latest suit styles but now were just a tad threadbare, sat patiently inside the coach fanning themselves. An escort dismounted, dutifully walked over, and helped the passengers step down. One passenger was considerably overweight and definitely in need of assistance. Without it, he might have split the seams in his already ill-fitting duds. The slenderer of the two nodded deferentially to the escort who'd helped him disembark and scowled at me. Obviously, we were not getting off to a good start to whatever they had in mind. I expect the heat did little to improve their attitudes. "My name is Tubbs. This here is Mr. Burke. Which of you is Mr. O'Toole?" the slender man demanded more than asked.

I tipped my hat. "Howdy. I'm Jack O'Toole," I responded. "Pleasure to meet you, Mr. Tubbs." I extended my hand, but he rejected my hospitality. I felt that he would have spit on my hand if given the chance. "Welcome to Rising Cross Ranch." I forced a smile.

"You ever own slaves, O'Toole?"

"No." I glanced at three of the uniformed police escorts who happened to be black. The emotions revealed in their eyes spoke volumes of anger, suspicion, resentfulness, and even vengeance. I felt as though they'd like nothing better than to put a serious beating on a White man. "We never owned slaves. In fact, we helped some escape slavery."

Blue Flower stepped from our front door. "Do we have guests, Jack?"

Upon seeing an Indian woman, Tubbs's eyes widened. He was no Indian lover. He wrote something in a small notebook. "That your squaw?" he said derisively.

"Blue Flower is my wife. My children are inside."

"Bunch of breeds, eh?" Tubbs said rhetorically.

I was already forming what might be described as

quite ungodly judgments about these men, especially Tubbs. "What's your business here, Mr. Tubbs?" I demanded in an attempt to steer the discussion to the situation at hand.

"You willing to sign a loyalty oath to the Union?" Tubbs asked perfunctorily while eyeing Blue Flower.

"To the United States of America?" I responded, as I strove to suppress my growing anger. I rightly figured it wouldn't do to wipe out an official government contingent.

"Yea. To that," offhanded Tubbs.

"Why should I have to?"

"The government says so."

"Or what?" I persisted.

"We seize your property," replied Tubbs.

Burke took a swig from a bottle and belched. He nurtured a large tobacco chaw in his cheek and spat an ugly mass of brown junk into Rising Cross dust.

I looked askance at him.

He belched again.

Tubbs coughed to get my attention. "You going to sign this?"

"What does it get me?"

"Like I said, O'Toole. The government won't seize your property."

"Y'all care for coffee?" called a smiling Blue Flower from the gallery.

Tubbs and Burke exchanged curious looks. They'd hardly expected any hospitality given their mission. "Er, thanks," Tubbs managed to blurt.

I gave an assuring nod to Buck and Hardy. They eased their hands from the butts of their revolvers, and I saw Shorty over beside the barn lower the business end of his rifle.

Blue Flower brought out a pot and poured coffee into the waiting cups of the mounted escorts. She even served the coach driver.

Tin cups seemed to magically appear in Tubbs's and Burke's hands. "Right kind, Mr. O'Toole," managed Tubbs.

I saw Buck shake his head ever-so-slightly as he watched me defuse a potentially ugly situation.

I relieved Tubbs of the document he'd waved in front of me and signed it. "Y'all are free to let your horses drink over yonder," I offered with a motion to the water trough. By now, Henry rifles had disappeared into saddle scabbards.

"Thanks kindly, Mr. O'Toole." Tubbs seemed relieved. I reckoned that he'd met with some stiff resistance in performing his rather distasteful duties, and this day had turned out to be a relief.

I saw that Tubbs had a slight lean to his left, as though one leg was shorter. "You do some fighting, Mr. Tubbs?"

He nodded. "Fought for McClellan at Gettysburg. Took a ball in my knee," he revealed.

"Well, thanks for serving, Mr. Tubbs."

That seemed to further bolster his spirits. For me, I was just striving to get beyond the aftermath of what had been a terrible war that rocked the very soul of the nation.

With the document signed and niceties at an end, Tubbs and Burke waited to be assisted back into the coach. Before he stepped up, he turned and looked over at Blue Flower. "Much obliged for the coffee, Mrs. O'Toole," he said with a friendly smile. He proceeded to make his way into the coach, giving me a grateful nod as they headed away.

FIFTEEN
RUSTLERS

RECONSTRUCTION TURNED out to be a rather poor term to use in describing the next few years in Texas. Confronting hatred, deception, bitterness, hostility, and wickedness, among other evils, had become a far-too-frequent occurrence. We hoped that Texas would soon rejoin the Union, though that alone wouldn't resolve the lawlessness.

The war had spawned bands of lawless men. We heard news of lawbreakers like the James brothers and Younger brothers that had ridden with the guerrilla leader William Quantrill then stuck to their evil ways after the war's end.

We stuck with our long-held policy of never venturing out alone. We acquired an additional ten thousand acres, Shorty led another trail drive north, and operations at Rising Cross were smooth as silk—mostly. Will's and Kate's family was growing as were Isaac's and Sarah's. Blue Flower and I suffered through the loss of a baby girl at birth. It was a sad event, but we'd been blessed with four children, and our oldest were chiding us constantly for more grown-up tasks. Isa, George, and Peter yearned to join me on hunts.

"It is time," advised Blue Flower over breakfast. She had been preparing our sons for this time.

I nodded. "I'm ready." I knew this day would come. It meant spending a greater portion of my days with my sons, instructing them in skills that would serve them well as grown men. We would hunt, fashion traps and become expert with weapons, study the ways of the wildlife, understand the messages of the trail, discover poultices that would save their lives, and learn the languages of the horse. I would pass on all that Spirit Talker taught me, and it would all barely scratch the surface of what must be learned. I decided that making their own weapons would be a good beginning, as I could lecture and grow their knowledge of the frontier before we fully undertook the rigors of hunting or trapping.

The boys must have anticipated the moment, as they emerged from their room with excitement written large across their faces. "We're ready, Pa," declared Isa. He was the boldest of the three—always leading George and Peter into whatever was to be pursued. Nadua had gotten old enough that she could tease the boys into doing foolish acts that would earn a tongue-lashing from their mother. But it worked both ways. Isa was good for dropping a toad down the back of poor Nadua's dress or scaring her with a snake.

"What shall we do, Pa?" echoed George.

"Before you can hunt, you must make your own weapons," I advised. "Today, you will begin to make your own bows." I knew of a nearby stand of junipers from which excellent bows could be crafted.

My sons gazed disappointedly at me, as though they'd reckoned to begin by my taking them hunting.

I smiled. "You want to hunt? Fetch your bows and arrows." Of course, they had only the most rudimentary of weapons, fit only as toys.

They reluctantly nodded their understanding.

"We're going to ride out to the stand of junipers to the east. We'll find suitable wood and begin making beautiful bows that will serve you for many years."

———

BUCK SADDLED up and joined us. I was still wary of possible trouble. The Kiowas and Utes were riled up, and I remained concerned about rogue state policemen. My younger brother Buck provided us with an extra adult to defend against attack.

We were inspecting the junipers for the best candidates for bow making, when Buck happened to look off to our west. "Jack! What's going on out there?" He pointed to four men driving a couple of dozen cattle across our range.

I paused my lecture about the characteristics of juniper that made the wood great for bows and pulled a telescope from my saddlebag. I lifted the spyglass to my eye, aimed it where Buck had pointed, and brought it into focus.

"Rustling right under our noses," observed Buck.

I found myself in a bit of a quandary. With the boys along, I dared not place them in any danger, and they sure weren't ready for any grown-up gunplay.

The boys displayed a mix of youthful excitement and abject fear. They looked to me for what to do.

"Buck, skirt wide and fetch Hardy, Shorty, and Will. I'm going to keep an eye on the rustlers for so long as I can." I reckoned to keep an eye on them and take them on only if they threatened us. This would also enable me to protect my sons. I drew the Sharps from its scabbard. I was confident in hitting a target at upward of several hundred yards but prayed not to be called to do that. I pulled my .44 caliber 1860 Colt Army revolver. The slug packed a serious wallop. I looked at each of my sons. I'd taken them target shooting a handful of times, but there was a huge difference between hitting an inanimate target and a human. "Isa, take this. Do not use it unless I tell you." Isa was the best marksman of the three. George and Peter showed disappointment, but understood.

I stood beside Big Red and kept my telescope aimed at the rustlers. Roughly a half hour passed. Blessedly, the gang was dealing with a couple of ornery beeves. The gang looked anxious to herd their stolen prizes away, but it was slow going thus far.

"What you figuring to do, Pa?" asked Isa.

"Waiting for our hands," I responded. There was no point in hiding the truth. I wasn't going to take on four men of unknown ability by myself. "You should never do anything foolish." It was a fact, a lesson to be taught and learned. "Just stay low." As the last word rolled from my tongue, I saw a rustler tumble from his horse, then heard the report of a distant rifle.

The three remaining rustlers were now on high alert. I saw outlaw rifles being brought into play and gunsmoke as they were fired in the direction of the shot that felled the first man.

"Should we help, Pa?" asked Isa.

"Just stay put. We'll be reinforcements if needed."

My sons immediately recognized that they had an important role, though it was unlikely that action would come our way. I spoke too soon.

A blue-gray haze of gunsmoke hung over the herd. Two rustlers had been shot from their saddles, and the two remaining lawbreakers decided that retreat was their best and only viable option. Upon seeing the stand of junipers, they decided to head my way.

They were perhaps hallway to the position occupied by me and my boys, when they realized that we were there. With Shorty, Buck, Hardy, Isaac, Will, and even Perez on their tails, the Guadalupe River to their left, and an open range to their right, they had little choice but to charge onward toward the trees.

"Hug the ground, boys," I directed my sons to lie low. I kneeled and brought the Sharps carbine to my shoulder. I had to be accurate, as I didn't want an errant slug hitting my brother or one of our hands. The rustlers were about fifty yards away and charging head-on toward my position. I aimed and squeezed off a round. One rustler spun from the saddle, sorely wounded. The remaining thief pulled up with arms raised high. My homemade posse quickly surrounded him.

Shorty and Hardy mounted the wounded rustler back onto his cayuse. They led them to me, stopping twenty or so feet away from me and pulling them roughly from their mounts. The two were checked for weapons and then pushed and prodded to me. They were forced to their knees, where they cowered. The wounded man had even wet his pants.

Isa, George, and Peter were wide-eyed at the show unfolding before them. I had a teaching opportunity ahead of me. First, I retrieved my Colt revolver from Isa. We didn't need an accident.

I was physically a lot larger than the rustlers, and that of itself was an intimidating factor.

"Who are you?" It was an easy enough question.

The rustler who'd surrendered was tight-lipped despite his obvious fear. The wounded cattle thief was in considerable pain. "Gordie W-w-wills," he stammered. "Help me. I be bleedin' out."

Shorty strode up behind Wills and examined the wound. He rolled his eyes. "He'll live, boss."

"Think he can handle a haircut?" I asked.

"Shucks, boss. The last rustler we scalped didn't see the next day."

Total fear swept Wills's face.

"Shut yer pie hole, Gordie. They ain't gonna scalp nobody," declared the other rustler.

I glanced at my boys and turned my head so the rustlers couldn't see me wink. I put my finger to my mouth to ensure them being silent. "Well, Mr. Wills. Why are you trying to rustle Rising Cross cattle? Someone paying you?"

Wills spat into the dirt beside him. "Booger Salido put us up to it," he revealed.

"You dummy," said his fellow rustler.

I turned to him. "For a man who's seen two of his fellow cattle thieves shot dead and another wounded, you keep showing off how downright stupid you are. When we turn you in to the sheriff in Bandera and you face the judge, your fate is sealed. I am thinking that a rope might be too good for you." I laid an angry look on him. "Who is Booger Salido?" I asked, as I slid my Bowie knife from its sheath. By now, Zeb had found his way to my side. The appearance of a large wolf seemed to do special wonders in loosening even the most reluctant tongues.

"Tye Wicker. My name is Tye Wicker," said the rustler, as his eyes grew wide as a shard of sunlight bounced from my knife's cold steel edge. "Salido...he be Mexican."

I'd heard about this game, though it had been happening closer to the Rio Grande. Mexicans would steal Texas cattle, overbrand them, and then sell them back to other Texas ranchers. Perversely, it worked both ways. Cattle not sold would be killed for their hides. It was a right-profitable enterprise—illegal but profitable. The good news for these two rustlers was that it was unlikely they'd been paid in advance. While this Salido fellow would not likely hunt them down, we would see to their fates.

"You turnin' us in?" asked Wills.

I shook my head. "Any reason I shouldn't?" I looked up to see a couple of buzzards already circling over the bodies of the other two rustlers. Zeb emitted a low growl. "I could just leave you to my furry friend here.

"I got a woman an' two kids," pleaded Wills.

Well, didn't that beat all. "And you figured rustling cattle would help them?" I replied to his entreaty. There was no reason here for any sort of compromise, no reasoning things out. A hanging offense had been committed.

"Dirk put us up to it. Owed him gamblin' money," confessed Wills. "D-d-dang but this arm hurts, sir."

I hadn't heard from Wicker yet, but Wills was surely headed down an ever-widening path of evil. That he might be telling the truth about a family, was gut-wrenching but not swaying my thinking. "Hardy, ride to the river and find some woolly lamb's ear. Spirit Talker taught me that the leaves make a great poultice. We'll bandage Mr. Wills's arm." I turned to Wicker. "Shorty, tie his hands behind his back, and you and Will set him set back on his horse."

Wicker struggled to resist, but Shorty was the stronger man by far. "Señor Salido...he be comin' fer yuh," he growled. Shorty tied the rustler's wrists tighter. He and Will set him on his horse. Shorty winked at Will across the saddle. "Whatcha think, Will? Got a noose?"

Wicker spat again. "Y'all ain't hangin' me," he sneered with misplaced confidence.

I caught on quickly. "Hardy, do you think you, Buck, and Shorty can cart these lawbreakers to Sheriff Garrison in Fredericksburg without a necktie party?" I wanted them turned over to the sheriff, as I held no trust for the state police. I missed Maier, but a succession of sheriffs had followed him, and Garrison was now the Gillespie County sheriff. "Will, please bring the buckboard and see to burying those bodies out there. Pack their personal effects to send to Fredericksburg with these two." I didn't figure to encumber Hardy with carting the moldering bodies to Fredericksburg, as they'd stink to high heaven and serve to attract unwanted animal guests. Besides, there was no sense unnecessarily burdening the sheriff.

The boys soon formed up a column that was more of a grim procession that included the two remaining rustlers and the two draped over their horses' saddles. Will and Buck saw to herding our longhorns back to their grazing. I wasn't certain I'd ever meet this Salido fellow that Wicker talked about, but I found it hard to imagine him covering three hundred miles to avenge perceived wrongs to these ne'er-do-wells. I surely couldn't be worried about it. There were plenty of real threats around. It was up to me and folks like me to cast light to push back against the darkness of evil.

By now, Isa, George, and Peter had likely seen enough to scare the wits out of little Nadua with stories of what their pa had done. Importantly, they'd seen me upholding the law. Rustling was a hanging offense, but I was no judge and jury and it was for the court to decide punishment. We stood and watched Shorty lead the silent procession away.

"Let's cut some juniper, boys," I chided.

"But you have a saw, Pa," noted Isa.

"The Comanche had no saws. Use the hatchet." I was determined to have the boys fashion their bows in as traditional a manner as possible, beginning with cutting their own wood with the hatchet. The hatchet was as close as I had to a tomahawk.

We soon had the wood we needed, mounted up, and headed home. It was past midday when we arrived.

"What take long?" queried Blue Flower. "Food ready."

Isa was bust-a-button proud at what he'd observed. "Pa had to chase off some cattle thieves," he said matter-of-factly.

Blue Flower smiled. Now she understood why Shorty and the others had ridden off in such an all-fired hurry.

"Ana o'a hi'it," I said.

"*Ana o'a hi'it,*" echoed the boys, mimicking their pa.

We were soon seated around the kitchen table, savoring Blue Flower's delectable goodies. The boys took turns relating all that had transpired with the rustlers. I reckoned they'd get ever-better at storytelling, as my involvement was embellished to an embarrassing degree.

———

MAKING bows and then arrows was a laborious but ultimately satisfying process. The boys were justly proud of having crafted weapons that I was sure Spirit Talker would have admired. They were easily the match for the bow I'd made years back under Spirit Talker's teaching and used to this day. They initially complained at chipping flint arrowheads, since steel tips could be bought. The result turned out to be well worth the effort, as the boys admired their handiwork.

The true test lay ahead. We spent a couple of weeks practicing against targets I'd cut out to resemble deer and other game. My sons were soon impressed at the power with which a bow could deliver an arrow. They'd doubted that a shaft could be shot clean through a deer until I took them on the first hunt with their very own bows. While we practiced, I regaled them with instructions on moving silently through various environments to be encountered, such as leaf-covered forest trails versus prairies versus rocky landscapes. There was no substitute for actually heading out to the trails to hunt the abundant wildlife that so attracted us. Roast venison steaks, buffalo ribs, lean antelope meat, or fatty wild hog all tempted the taste buds. I even cooked up a rattlesnake we'd found in the barn. Around the Texas hills, snake was almost a diet staple.

We sat quietly in a thicket. Having seen a small herd of deer, we snuck to this spot as close as we dared. I signed to the boys that we were downwind. The deer couldn't smell us but could hear and see well enough, so we needed to be especially stealthy. I motioned toward the nearby stream. They'd soon be moving to its trickling waters to slake their thirst. They'd be a mere twenty feet from us.

We sat still and quiet for better than an hour. Patience was less about being taught than it was about being experienced. My youngest son Peter especially wanted to move.

Finally, the deer made their way to the creek. I ever-so-slowly drew an arrow from my quiver and nocked it to the bowstring. A buck with impressive antlers surveilled the area. I decided that he was too impressive to kill. Better that he spawns equally majestic offspring. I moved my aim to a far less impressive buck standing a little closer. I pulled back the bowstring and let fly. The arrow drove clean through the buck's chest and embedded in a tree beyond him. Upon realization of the threat to them, the startled herd leaped away. The big buck wasted no time leading the flight.

"Pa, you shot him clean through!" exclaimed George.

And so the next year was filled with all manner of teachings and experiences. I made certain that they appreciated that we were taking the bounty as offered by God.

———

WE WERE BEGINNING to harbor faith that peace might have come at last. Peace did finally come to one member of our family. I was preparing to ride out to our western range, when Spirit Talker appeared with Prairie Flower and a ten-warrior escort. As he dismounted and we embraced, I felt a tension.

"Buffalo Hump go to Taa Narumi."

"Taa Narumi will be pleased to take him," I said by way of condolence.

"We go to Oklahoma." Spirit Talker looked longingly over his shoulder.

I had the sense that there was more. My Comanche brother was not telling me everything.

Blue Flower, having spotted her brother through a window, came running to greet him. "Mukwooru!

Come *ana o'a hi'it,*" she said, inviting him to eat with us.

Spirit Talker shook his head. "*Ap kooitu,*" he sadly declared.

Tears began to stream down Blue Flower's cheeks.

I'd never seen her cry.

"We go Oklahoma," shared Spirit Talker with her.

"Bury *ap?*" Blue Flower asked.

Spirit Talker sighed. "To live." It had been inevitable. Of all the Comanche, only the famed Quahadi Comanche Quanah Parker still remained free, and his days were likely numbered as his band dwindled from disease and the White's failure to meet treaty obligations ensuring sufficient food.

Blue Flower looked at me. Much as she longed to go to her father's burial place, she knew it wasn't feasible. Oklahoma was a long way through still-hostile territory. A safe return would be highly risky at best. "*Ana o'a hi'it,*" she persisted.

Spirit Talker finally gave in and motioned Prairie Flower and their two children to join them. He was about to send his warriors off, when I stopped him.

"We will feed all," I said firmly. "*Ana o'a hi'it!*" I shouted out to the Comanche warriors.

We spent the next couple of hours filling our home with a mix of English and Comanche coupled with a bit of Spanish from Perez, who'd come from the bunkhouse to help cook. The children quickly joined in play.

Blue Flower's father had passed away. Buffalo Hump had lived a long and productive life. He'd been a highly respected warrior and chief among the Comanche people, having first gained notoriety leading hundreds of warriors in 1840 through the heartland of Texas to the Gulf, burning Linnville and seriously damaging Victoria before returning home. He sought peace with the *tosas* several times, but treaties weren't worth the paper they'd been written on. Buffalo Hump had finally made peace with the Whites and spent his last days up in Oklahoma Territory. By virtue of marrying his daughter, I had gotten to know him quite well. He was a man of honor who felt deeply for his family. While he never came to know Christ, he respected the Christian faith that his son and daughter had accepted. We honored his passing with prayer.

Too soon, Spirit Talker readied to depart. They had a long journey ahead, and he hoped the state police wouldn't bother them. We would miss the times we had together in the Pedernales River country. Goodbye hugs were long and far too inadequate. I wasn't certain I'd ever see my Comanche brother again. It had been fifteen years since I'd saved him from an attacking mountain lion. We were older, and hopefully, wiser. We had come to more fully know God, even to enduring a Cheyenne attack during our baptism by George Freeman in the frigid waters of the North Platte River. My love for and marriage to his sister had cemented our family legacies, never to be parted.

We waved until all we saw of them on the horizon were specks of dust.

SIXTEEN
TOUGH DECISIONS

I HAD to admit that I was getting an itch that needed scratching. The past years had brought plenty of adventure as we built Rising Cross Ranch while dealing with all manner of challenges. Our good friend George Freeman had recently sent a letter noting that Wyoming, having officially become a territory back in 1868, was dealing with the dual phenomena of gold miners and oilmen. While men seeking instant fortunes mining for gold had become ever more common across various parts of our nation, oil exploration was more recent and was less about individuals digging or panning than larger enterprises extracting *black gold* from the bowels of the earth. Turned out that in 1862 a fellow named Alexander Cassidy had purchased a claim to a place called Oil Spring, from which oil seeped at a rate of one to three barrels a day. The Southern Utes had used oil for medicinal and body paint applications by skimming it from the layer it formed over nearby streams. A man named Gabriel Bowen who was looking for lead for bullets, first staked Oil Spring, but his claim was jumped by a chiseler named Dunn who gave it up stemming from charges related to rustling. That left Cassidy to develop the claim and sink the first oil wells. It didn't take long for enterprising men to consider the possibility of oil in Wyoming, Nebraska, and the Dakota Territory. From what I was able to learn, men would locate oil seeps like Oil Spring and go about drilling close by. Freeman wanted to know whether I might be interested in the oil business. Having rejected gold mining, I wasn't inclined to undertake the risks associated with oil. My reasoning was pretty much the same: I thrived on dealing with animals, living, breathing creations. Neither gold nor oil satisfied that lust. Bottom line, my itch still needed scratching.

I decided to ask my old friend August Klappenbach what he thought I should do, so I piled Blue Flower and our children into a buckboard, and with Buck and Hardy as escorts, headed to Bandera. For the family, it was a special treat, as Blue Flower had learned to love shopping, and the boys and Nadua had discovered candy.

While everyone else shopped, I cornered Klappenbach. "I'm feeling the need to expand my efforts at Rising Cross, August."

"Find any gold?" he asked with a laugh.

"No, and my friend in Wyoming already suggested oil," I responded with a serious expression.

"You might have a bigger problem ahead, Jack." He floated the words out and let them lay on the table between us.

I gave him an inquisitive look.

"I hear tell that a fellow named Booger Salido is itching to meet you."

It apparently had taken a couple of months for word of his failed Texas Hill Country cattle enterprise to reach him, and Salido was none too pleased. Wicker and Wills had paid the ultimate price for their errant ways, but apparently, good rustling help was tough to find even among the war veteran rabble of post-war Texas. "I reckoned we'd eventually hear something of him, though I hadn't expected it so soon."

Klappenbach stroked his now-bearded chin. "Well, some fools making use of those danged camels from Camp Verde encountered Salido north of Corpus Christi and said he was boasting of wanting to meet the fool who'd dared stop his cattle enterprise."

I sighed. "Evil is as evil does," I postulated. When would all the senseless evil end?

"*Hablas Español*? Teased Klappenbach.

"*Un poco*," I responded with a knowing grin. "And Comanche, some Lakota, and bits of Kiowa." I shook my head. There simply was no escape.

"I'd keep buying up land, Jack. Shucks, somebody might eventually even find oil on it." He took a sip from the coffee Stella had served. "You could venture north, but I don't expect you'll find life up there a whole lot different. Meanwhile, the railroads are opening new railheads and looking to ship beeves eastward. You'll have a thriving cattle business for years to come, Jack."

Nodding, I sipped my coffee. "Maybe it's time I took Blue Flower and our children on an adventure, August. We just might meet up with Spirit Talker and persuade him and Prairie Flower to join us. I'm curious about the country in Colorado."

"Well, go for it while you're young, Jack. I'm stuck here. Business is coming back, and I reckon to establish a bank. Bandera will be booming right quick."

———

HEADING BACK to Rising Cross I'm afraid I wasn't much fun. My thoughts were heavy with our future. Nadua and the boys were pleased to have ample quantities of the prized candies, Blue Flower had found a new dress and the various notions she needed, and Buck and Hardy were overjoyed at having purchased new tack and each a mighty fine set of duds. Me? I was wondering if and when I might meet Booger Salido and how to best expand Rising Cross Ranch.

I'd ridden point for the final couple of miles leading to the ranch. I was rightly pleased at the dozens of healthy beeves dotting our pastures. My eyes couldn't miss the fancy silver-studded black saddle on the incredibly fine stallion hitched in front of our house.

Sitting on a bench smoking a cigar was one of the most gaudy, lavishly dressed men I'd ever seen. His dark blue jacket and pants with intricate embroidered decorations set off a white silk shirt with gold string tie, polished black boots featuring spurs with large rowels, a nickel-plated Colt revolver hung from a black leather holster, and a very wide-brimmed hat decorated with dangles and embroidery. Cigar smoke curled around his black hair and the thin mustache situated under an aquiline nose crowned by a pair of dark steely eyes. And he was so skinny he might barely have qualified to serve as a fence rail. I paused, oblivious to the racket of the buckboard driven behind me to the front of our house. Given the man's appearance, I guessed he was Mexican. Could this be the Booger Salido I'd been warned about?

"¿Señor O'Toole?" called the decidedly slender gentleman as he arose from the bench and purposefully strode to the edge of the gallery with a jangle of spurs. "*Buen día, estoy Benito Gustavo Verde de Sallido.*" He bowed gracefully.

I slid from Big Red's saddle. "Howdy, I'm Jack O'Toole. Welcome to Rising Cross Ranch."

The buckboard groaned to a stop behind me in a cloud of dust, and the boys leaped out and headed to the bunkhouse to share candy with cowboys that hadn't gone to Bandera with us. Blue Flower climbed down with Nadua in tow and stood alongside me. Hardy and Buck normally would have unloaded the wagon, but now stood aside with hands hovering over pistol butts. As was his habit, Zeb appeared. He especially got Salido's attention.

"This is my wife, Blue Flower, and two of my cowboys. *¿Viajas solo?*" I mixed in a touch of what little Spanish I knew to determine if he traveled alone. I knew it was unlikely but had to ask.

Salido nodded deferentially to Blue Flower, Hardy, and Buck. "*Tengo seis pistoleros,*" he matter-of-factly informed me. I hadn't a clue where his six gunmen might be hidden.

I sought to be friendly. "*¿Café?*" I offered.

Salido smiled broadly, showing pearly-white teeth. "*Si, es bueno.*" He gave a suspicious look at Zeb. He apparently had become aware that Zeb was no domestic dog.

Blue Flower understood my attempt at hospitality. She walked past Salido, giving him a don't-mess-with-us look before entering our house.

"*¿Hablas inglés?*" I asked.

"*Un poco,*" he responded with a certain coyness that led me to believe he knew more than a little.

"What brings you to Rising Cross?" I inquired.

"*Cuatro hombres murieron,*" he answered. "Salido not happy." He was lamenting the loss of four rustlers, but more likely, the potential profit their failure had cost him.

As I looked up at him, I became aware of my physical advantage, though a revolver might quickly cancel that. I gave him a hard look. "Your *hombres* tried to steal my cattle, my *ganado*."

I think he was impressed that I showed no weakness. Salido may have had six gunmen hidden somewhere, but by now, Shorty, Will, and my other hands would be standing ready for any incident requiring gunplay. Salido's eyes shifted to Zeb. That was a mistake. It's bad practice to try to stare down a wolf.

Zeb bared his fangs and let out a low growl.

"*¿Qué es lobo?*" asked Salido.

"Su nombre es Zeb. Regalo de Dios."

He nodded. "*¿Crees en Dios?*" Salido asked whether I believed in God.

"And Christ is my Savior," I assured him.

Salido paused to think on all of this. It was quite clear that nothing was going as he had planned.

Blue Flower appeared with a pot of coffee and three cups.

I was curious as to the three, but then she poured herself coffee after serving me and Salido.

"Blue Flower Penateka Comanche, daughter of Buffalo Hump, might chief." She gave Salido a look that would have lifted his scalp had it been a knife. She was daring him to mess with us. "Comanche call Jack O'Toole Pohya Isa, Walks With Wolves. Strong *sunipu!*" She hissed the last word for emphasis.

I saw Perez poke his head in a window. He'd apparently advised her to act boldly with the likes of Salido.

Salido didn't know what to make of Blue Flower. Between my strong wife and Lobo companion, he necessarily found himself becoming less aggressive. If he had any threatening plan, it had broken down by now. *"Hacer negocios,"* he said with a turn to me. He was proposing to do some business.

"Estoy escuchando." I told him that I was listening.

"Salido comprar ganado." He smiled. "Pagar con oro."

He sure had my curiosity aroused. He'd shifted from shady cattle rustler to cattle buyer, offering to buy my cattle with gold. I thought back to how this was a long way from the days when I worried about Confederate script. *"¿Cuánto?"*

"Sesenta dólares por cabeza," he said without hesitation.

Salido's offer was just about the going price for a three-year-old steer. I'd received fifty-five dollars a head, so his offer of sixty was generous. Payment in gold made it irresistible. *"¿Cuántas cabezas de ganado?"* I asked.

"Trescientos," he responded.

I quickly did the math in my head. Eighteen thousand dollars in gold was a handsome piece of change. "You have the *dinero*, the *oro*?" I pressed.

Salido grinned. *"El dinero está en el banco."*

"¿Dónde?" I inquired.

"Está en Brownsville," Salido said it, knowing that Brownsville was a long way from Rising Cross Ranch. Now, I found myself anticipating a request that I'd already seen coming.

"Jack *conducir ganado a México,"* ventured Salido. Salido moved from the gallery into the open yard, and I unthinkingly did so as well.

Blue Flower appeared to casually lean against the doorframe as she sipped her coffee.

Salido was expecting me to trust him. A man with a flourishing rustling operation expected me to drive three hundred of my beeves south to be paid in gold but quite likely to be stolen by his very own *vaqueros*. This man had the audacity to imply that he was a man of faith. It was part of his game.

My mind churned with possibilities. I glanced knowingly at Hardy and Buck, then responded to Salido. *"Nueve mil dólares ahora y nueve mil cuando entregamos Ganado."* My Spanish was improving. Salido would have to give me half the money before I'd move a single longhorn to Mexico.

Salido shook his head. His game was up, and he knew it. His hand moved toward the Colt revolver at his hip, but the click of two hammers being cocked behind him caused him to pause, making such a foolish move. Blue Flower stood with both shotgun barrels ready to fire. Salido exhaled and shrugged. His choices were ugly and uglier. He'd been beaten.

It was a standoff. Or was it? I caught Salido make a nearly imperceptible glance toward the barn. Some of his *pistoleros* were likely hidden behind it. But likely not all of them. My suspicion was correct. One of his men had climbed onto our roof. His drooping mustache, sombrero, white loose-fitting shirt, and single bandolier graced a lithe form in the process of raising a rifle to his shoulder. He levered a round and aimed at me.

An evil grin crossed Salido's lips. He nodded ever-so-slightly.

The yard erupted in gunfire. Salido's *pistoleros* charged from behind the barn and ran into a fusillade from Shorty and my hands. The *pistolero* on the roof squeezed off a round, but it was high, as an arrowhead suddenly protruded from his chest. The Mexican leader himself moved to his gun, but a buckshot exploded behind him and blew into his back. Zeb was on him as he fell face-first into the Texas dust. It was an ugly scene that lasted no more than five seconds at most. The yard was littered with dead and wounded Mexicans.

I pulled Zeb off Salido and glanced at Blue Flower. She was calmly reloading the shotgun. Salido groaned. He was dying. *"Yanqui muy inteligente,"* he managed to cough out.

I kicked his gun away. Then, I looked up on the roof at the dead *pistolero*. Where had an arrow come from?

Isa emerged from the side of the house carrying his new bow and a handful of arrows. He was trembling. The expression on his young face bore the look of utter horror at what he had done.

"Pa!"—he cried—"I had to, Pa." He ran to me and buried his face in my chest. Growing up can come awful hurriedly.

I pushed him away at arms-length with my hands firmly gripping his shoulders. "Look at me, Isa," I said as gently as I could muster. He looked up through baleful eyes. "You did the right thing." It wasn't quite the time for a speech on when it was okay to kill a human. I prayed he'd never have to do it again, but this was the western frontier, and it was highly likely he might be called to repeat the often-burdensome task of taking a human life. Still, it didn't seem right for a thirteen-year-old boy to kill a man. Then again, who was I to judge? I was only fifteen when I had to kill a man.

Blue Flower stood on the gallery watching Isa and me. She smiled approvingly.

George and Peter finally emerged from the house. Both were armed, but had not followed in Isa's aggressive footsteps. "Isa, you were awesome," gushed Peter, expressing both boys' admiration for Isa's deed.

Then, the boys saw Salido lying face down in the dust with his back torn to ribbons and his leg mangled from

Zeb's fearsome jaws. Blue Flower tried to hide the shot-gun, but she was too late. The still-smoking muzzle gave her away. "Ma?" exclaimed George.

I diverted their attention. "Isa, go inside and get cleaned up, then you, George, and Peter come back out here to help." I didn't want the boys' minds dwelling on the dead *pistolero* on our roof or Salido himself.

I finally locked eyes with Blue Flower. I mouthed, "I love you." She'd saved me before from a Comanche shaman. My beautiful but tough Comanche wife was surely a gift to me from God.

Shorty, Buck, and the other cowboys rounded up the wounded *pistoleros* and herded them to me. The three Mexicans had received serious gunshots, but only one man's wounds were life-threatening. "What shall we do with these, boss?" asked Shorty.

"Will and Buck, bind the wounds of those two. They likely don't speak English, so get Perez to interpret. Shorty and Hardy, gather the personal effects of the dead men, then haul the bodies to that juniper grove east of here and give them a decent Christian burial." I felt a Christian interment was undeserved, but my nature was to try to think the best of even the most evil folks. We knew nothing of these men's lives back in Mexico. Did they have families? The question remained of what to do with the three wounded survivors, though it could soon be only two men considering that the severely wounded *pistolero* had bled profusely and was near his final breaths. It wasn't long before he joined Salido among the junipers.

I turned to my sons. "Go fetch the buckboard, boys, and hitch up the team." I reckoned that the wounded *pistoleros* were in no condition to ride to Fredericksburg, given the nature of their wounds. It's tough to sit a horse for any length of time, but especially with the lower body gunshot wounds these men had received.

———

ON A HUNCH, I decided to accompany the prisoners to Fredericksburg. With the military-style government still in place, the fact that these men were Mexicans was concerning. I had no idea what Salido's status was south of the border. Over the years, there had been many altercations along the Rio Grande. Few rose to the level of being considered international incidents. The Texas Rangers dealt with incursions by Apache and Mexicans, usually involving cattle rustling, though the Indians were more inclined to lift a scalp or two from ranchers.

We treated the wounds of the two remaining *pistoleros*, tied their hands, and loaded them into the buckboard. Hardy and Buck would provide escort. It was a long enough ride, that I had Blue Flower pack some venison jerky for the prisoners.

SEVENTEEN

INTERNATIONAL INCIDENT

WE ROLLED into Fredericksburg under crystal-clear azure skies and sought out Sheriff Garrison's office first thing. I looked forward to making the lawman's acquaintance. I reckoned by turning over my prisoners and relating the story of the Mexican connection with the rustlers that had already graced his jail, my visit would be brief and leave time to buy supplies and visit with the McGregors. I reckoned wrong.

I climbed down from Big Red and knocked on Garrison's door.

"Come in," invited a voice from within.

I heard the scrape of a gun across a wooden surface, likely a desk. "Jack O'Toole here to pay a visit and deliver some lawbreakers, Sheriff."

"O'Toole? You the fellow that owns that big spread east of here. Got the squaw wife?" he responded. His aspersion toward Blue Flower didn't bode well.

"I've got two wounded Mexicans we captured after their attack on my ranch."

"Didn't a couple of your hands deliver a pair of rustlers just a bit ago?"

I nodded with an eye to the .44 caliber Colt sitting on Garrison's desk. "Seems those two were working for a fellow out of Mexico named Benito Salido. They rustled cattle that he'd sell back to Texas ranchers. The two I've brought you today were what Salido called his *pistoleros*."

"What of Salido?"

"Killed during their attack," I said flatly.

Garrison shook his head. "Seems the telegraph travels faster than your wagon, O'Toole. You've created what is called an international incident," he stated drolly.

"I've created a what?" I exclaimed.

"Salido was a man of money and power in Tamaulipas. He had *mucho* influence." Garrison gave an ironic chuckle. "How do you think he and his band of gunman made it from Brownsville to your spread without being stopped? He spread a little *dinero* around the countryside."

"So?" I asked.

"Well, you stirred up some trouble. I know it's not your fault, but the federal folks in Austin want a piece of you to make a show for the Mexicans." Garrison slipped his Colt back into its holster and stood.

"What about these *pistoleros*?" I pressed.

"They'll likely return them to Mexico as a show of good faith." Garrison shrugged. "It's not fair, but that's the way the show is being run."

By now, Hardy had walked in.

Garrison nodded to him. "Weren't you a Texas Ranger a few years back? Hardy Sullivan, isn't it?"

"Yes, that's true," responded Hardy.

"Sure could use some Texas Rangers these days.

Those state police aren't worth a hoot," observed Garrison.

I saw an opportunity to pull Garrison more to my side. "I met Hardy back when I was scouting for Rip Ford. Was with him at the Battle of Little Robe Creek back in '58."

"I appreciate y'all's service, but we still have this here international incident. I'm afraid you'll need to cart the two Mexicans to Austin. This is a federal matter and not in my jurisdiction." Garrison ushered us outside. "Sorry, gents."

———

WE WERE DISAPPOINTED, to say the least. We did stop at the general store and gathered a few supplies for the coming autumn season. These days, it was mostly flour, sugar, and ammunition. Meanwhile, the two *pistoleros,* whom we now knew as Ramone and Luis, were downright miserable. We managed to have a doctor in Fredericksburg treat their wounds, compliments of Will McGregor.

It was great to see Will and Colleen again, but we hustled out of town first thing in the morning. The trip home was drudgery, given that we were all-too-aware of possible difficulties ahead.

As we pulled into the yard at Rising Cross Ranch, the telltale carriage, the preferred transportation mode of Mr. Virgil Tubbs sat waiting for us. He'd brought his escort of six state police. "Welcome home, Mr. O'Toole," he called out as we approached.

Blue Flower stood on the gallery with our children protectively surrounding her. Even five-year-old Nadua looked ready to fight.

"What's your business here, Mr. Tubbs?" I challenged.

"We've come to arrest anyone who shot and killed the Señor Salido and his *vaqueros*," demanded Tubbs.

"*Vaqueros*? More properly, *pistoleros*, Mr. Tubbs. They were hired guns who attacked us."

"You will have a chance to prove that, O'Toole." Tubbs scanned the yard. He now faced nearly a dozen of my family and cowhands, all armed. "I'd be much obliged, if those that killed Señor Salido and his *vaqueros* would please step forward and surrender."

I shook my head. "There was a lot of lead flying around, Mr. Tubbs. Some of it theirs and some ours. We didn't keep track of who shot who."

"In that case, you're all under arrest," stated Tubbs unemotionally.

"Are your state policemen going to start shooting up our home, if we resist?" I was getting just a tad angry and struggling with my faith to keep calm.

"We'll do whatever is necessary, O'Toole." Tubbs smiled. He actually seemed to be enjoying this.

I looked at the state police mounted on the sorriest nags Texas likely was barely able to afford. "How many of you are ready to die trying to arrest us?"

They began to look nervously at each other and then to Tubbs. I can't say as they appeared ready to give up their lives for some vague quarrel with Mexico.

Tubbs snorted. "You win today, O'Toole. I'll be back and arrest the lot of you." He began to climb into the carriage, but paused to have one of the escorts help him in.

"You stooping to arresting women and children, Tubbs. What sort of human are you?"

Tubbs gave a sideways glance from his seat and

banged his walking stick on the carriage roof to signal the driver to move out.

As Tubbs and his contingent headed up the trail, I sighed. There were still two prisoners to deal with. It appeared that I had little choice but to head to Austin to get this mess behind us.

———

AS WE DROVE the heavily rutted road toward Austin, it brought back memories of moving escaped slaves to join the underground railroad we'd hidden within our cattle drives. It hadn't been much in terms of numbers, but I'd managed to guide a handful of slaves to freedom up north.

We had passed Sam Collins Circle C Ranch and were about midway on our journey when a familiar voice hailed us. Who should appear at trailside but Cutter Kincaid. His dwarfish body bore the scars wrought at the hands of Rowdy Sikes.

"Whar yuh headin'?" asked Kincaid.

I'd been riding point, gave a thumb over my shoulder to the wagon. "You're looking at a full-fledged international incident back there, Cutter." I quickly summarized what had led to our predicament.

Kincaid smiled broadly. "I kin take care of this," he assured me. "Jus' giv'em to me."

"What about Tubbs?" I expressed with concern.

Now Kincaid laughed heartily. "Tubbs!? Virgil Tubbs?!" His shout might have awakened the dead. "Why, I kin handle that sorry excuse fer a man."

Hardy, Buck, and I exchanged glances. Hardy nodded, and Buck shrugged. "What do you have in mind, Cutter?" I asked.

"Jus' leave them Mex's to me," he responded. "I'll get 'em snuck back in ole Mexico lickety-split." He looked at the two wounded bandits. "*Pistoleros,* my patootee." He slapped his thighs and laughed again.

The two *pistoleros* were reluctant to leave the relative safety of the buckboard, but a wave of my Bowie knife soon had them standing on unsteady legs. "Shall I leave their hands tied?"

Kincaid nodded. "Yep. Jus' fer now. They won't be runnin' off anywhere."

"Yes. They both took slugs where it hurts," I noted. "Likely won't be riding horses anytime soon."

We watched Kincaid poke and prod the *pistoleros* along ahead of him and soon disappear among the flora of the Texas prairie. We turned the wagon and headed home. I held great store in Cutter Kincaid's ability to take care of the two Mexicans and handle Tubbs. Nevertheless, I said a prayer asking God's protection. If Kincaid somehow was to fail in his disposal of the so-called international incident, life might get a tad nasty for us at Rising Cross Ranch.

———

WE HEARD nothing further from Tubbs or any of the folks in Austin. I was curious as to what Kincaid had done, but I'd have to await the next time our paths crossed.

I redoubled my teaching of my sons in the rigors and satisfactions entwined in practicing manly life skills. By the time a year had passed, I think the boys could have snuck up on a buffalo and tickled its posterior. Isa became incredibly accurate with the bow and arrow, while George and Peter were slightly better with the Sharps carbine.

For Christmas of 1871, I gifted each of the boys with .56 caliber Spencer repeating rifles. In fact, I was so impressed that I bought one for myself. While it lacked the firepower of the single-shot Sharps carbine, its ability to fire several rounds a minute made it an awesome weapon for defense as well as hunting. While weapons were a necessity on the Texas frontier, they were useless without the sets of skills necessary to properly use them. First and foremost was always asking the question of whether their use at a particular time was moral and truly necessary. Blue Flower and I had spent time instilling strong Godly values in the boys, so we felt that the boys were solidly rooted in biblical morality. It was in hunting, and if required, fighting that schooling was the toughest.

Isa's killing of the *pistolero* that was about to shoot me still hung heavy with him. He cornered me one evening after dinner. "Pa, can we talk?" He motioned toward the barn.

We strolled silently side-by-side to the barn. The night was chilly, so being inside its sheltering confines was welcome. "What's on your mind, Isa?" I asked.

"I feel the need to go on a vision quest," Isa stated quite flatly. He'd heard of the Comanche practice of going off alone to communicate with their god—in this case, our God—and listen for life instructions.

"This is good, son. I am proud of you. Do you know what you must do?" He was about to turn fifteen years old. He was a man so far as the frontier was concerned.

With a sheepish look, he admitted to having taken Spirit Talker aside and learned of the ritual. He hadn't yet shared it with George or Peter. This was okay, as the vision quest was a private matter to be undertaken in solitude only when ready.

"Go, my son. You shall be a light on this world." I found myself laying a heavy burden on his shoulders. But then, the yoke God placed on his servants was often heavy.

I was hopeful. While the darkness of war had loomed heavily, I saw brightness in our future. Isa would help deliver that light. My hand stroked Zeb as my thoughts drifted back to the life principles I'd striven to instill in my sons. Faith and trust in God was foremost, but the command God laid upon man in Genesis 1:28 always lingered deep in my soul. I strove to fill the earth and subdue it, to live a life of purpose that His creation would flourish. So it was that I'd overcome guilt, anger, and vengeance to save my dear Comanche brother Spirit Talker through mercy and forgiveness. It was the foundation of my seeking to overcome racial prejudice. I built Rising Cross Ranch not as a testament to wealth but as a means to exercise influence in the seats of government and among men who only yielded to power. I sought to motivate my sons by instilling joy, optimism, tranquility, love of God's physical creation, kindness, forgiveness, and benevolence, all exercised from a strength of body and soul. Consequently, they'd respected me and been willing to absorb all I could teach, to understand respecting and submitting to authority—especially God's —and to put into practice what they'd learned so as to meet all the challenges that life tossed their way. Thus, my confidence in Isa's going off on his vision quest was well-founded. Zeb licked my hand and nuzzled in close.

1872

WOLF'S TALE: THE BEGINNING

EIGHTEEN

VISION QUEST

I LOOKED out over the tops of the clouds as I sat wearing only a breechcloth. I'd chosen the highest spot I could find for my vision quest. The scene arrayed before me had me feeling as though I sat with God above the earth. My pa and ma had been right that I would find new purpose within myself. In fact, it would be my first true purpose as a man. I missed interaction with my brothers George and Peter, as we were close. It seemed strange that even my twin did not experience what I felt. Perhaps it was because it was my arrow and not one of his that had struck down the Mexican *pistolero*. It seemed to have forced me to grow up just a little faster. As twins, George and I would always have a special bond, but for this one difference.

I understood that the vision quest was sacred to the Comanche. No two were alike, as the vision quest was an individual endeavor. I sought to commune with the spirit world for life direction, in my case, God. Lingering in my early thoughts were biblical words shared by my pa to the effect that we should put to death what belongs to our worldly nature, such as sexual immorality, impurity, lust, evil desire, and greed. These were evils not to be tasted.

The first night was bone-chilling cold, mostly due to the cooling effect of a misty rain that fell for a couple of hours. I heard a coyote howl. The woolen blanket was barely sufficient to ward off the worst of the cold. I eventually lay on my side and fell asleep.

A dream? I felt a moist warmth on my face, then a tongue licked my cheek and was followed by a whimper. I cautiously opened one eye. The form that stood over me was silhouetted against the pinkish glow in the eastern sky just before sunrise. It was big and reminiscent of Pa's wolf, Zeb. My mind sought to catch up with the here and now. I opened both eyes and stared into what seemed like the biggest pair of blue eyes I'd ever seen. They were framed in gray fur and sat above a great set of fangs and dangling tongue that presently seemed to smile. It nudged me, as though it knew me and sought more response.

I sat up and reached my hand to stroke the wolf's fur. He didn't flinch but seemed to enjoy my touch. This was decidedly not wolf behavior, though I had grown up with Zeb and his unexpectedly tame responses to humans close to my pa. Zeb was quite intelligent, and I'd expect no less from any wolf. I couldn't help but feel that Zeb had something to do with my visitor. It may even have been one of his progeny.

The sun had just begun to crest the hills to the east. *Taabe*, the Comanche word for sun, shed its warming rays upon us. *Taabe*. The word stuck in my consciousness. Pa had said to be a light. It was all coming together. This was surely part of my vision quest. This great gray wolf had come to me in the light of dawn. I named him Taabe.

I ate some jerky and offered some to Taabe, but he refused. I understood. Wolves ate fresh kill, preferably their own prey. They didn't lower themselves in the food chain to be eaters of carrion. No, the wolf was an apex hunter, sharing the top place in the world of hunters with bears and mountain lions. Coyotes and others quailed in the presence of the wolf. Soon enough, Taabe ran off to hunt.

I resumed my meditation but was interrupted a few minutes later by Taabe's blue eyes staring at me as he gnawed on his fresh-killed breakfast. The rabbit never had a chance.

My thoughts strayed to my pa and ma. Was that supposed to happen? They had taught me much, yet I had much to learn. Where would my life path take me? I knew that I must follow the tougher, narrower path of faith that my folks had taught me. I must not only resist evil in myself but fight against it so much as I was able. If I was to be the light Pa called me to be, what form was that to take?

———

I SAT on the hilltop for three more days, drinking water and occasionally eating a small piece of jerky. My meditations were more prayers to God for guidance. He'd undoubtedly sent Taabe to me. What would He ask of me?

On the morning of my fourth day, I awakened to Taabe's urgent nudging. He'd push me, run off a few yards, and repeat the act. It was obvious that he was telling me something, or perhaps it was *He* telling me.

Taabe kept running in a northward direction. That was not the way to Rising Cross Ranch. I gathered my blanket and donned my buckskins and moccasins. I scanned the vicinity. My beloved pinto stallion. He'd been a wild horse that my pa had found up on the prairies way north of our ranch. I'd named him Paint, as the brown and black patches in his coat looked like someone had applied blotches of paint. He'd been dutifully grazing while waiting for me. I whistled to him, then buckled up my gun belt with my Colt revolver, picked up my Spencer rifle and bow and arrows, tossed my saddle over my shoulder, and headed for Paint. Taabe trotted along beside me, acting satisfied at having communicated the message that it was time to leave. The message? I was to head north to meet whatever God had laid out for me.

"You grow fat, Paint," I chided as I curried him before slipping on his bridle and saddle. Riding the frontier would quickly put him in prime traveling shape.

I had learned much about horsemanship from my pa and from Spirit Talker. The Comanche had a reputation as the most skilled horsemen of the Great Plains. No cavalry was their match. I'd heard endless after-dinner stories around our hearth of the Comanche in battle and of challenging hunts for game. The pony often spelled the difference between success in the hunt or in battle. Little wonder that the value of a Comanche warrior was measured not just in his wives and the feathers in his headdress but by the number of horses he owned. The chosen one, the pony a warrior invariably rides into battle, would be the one that joined with him as a single fighting force. Others were used for hunting and a few for trading. I felt a catch in my heart for the end of the Comanche empire that had once encompassed most of the southwest frontier of what is now the United States. Once numbering in the tens of thousands, they'd dwindled to a couple of thousand at best.

I checked my saddlebags. I'd pulled some jerky from one side at the beginning of my vision quest. Now, I checked the other side. Ma had stocked it with more jerky as well as pemmican, and Pa had slipped in a New Testament along with extra ammunition for the Spencer rifle. Digging deeper, I felt something wrapped in paper. I drew it out and just about burst into tears at what I held. It was a now stale but still edible bear sign. Such was her great love. Ties to my *numunahkahnis*, my family, were forever deeply embedded in my heart and soul. I nevertheless climbed into the saddle with a sigh and turned Paint toward Rising Cross Ranch. Taabe blocked my way. He stood across the trail with ears alert, then lowered his head and growled. Clearly, this was not the way—at least for now. I turned to the north, the direction Taabe had first indicated. He seemed joyful as he ran ahead of me.

I wondered what my pa and ma would think, yet I sensed that they expected that I would not return home from my vision quest. The truth had been spoken with the bear sign that Ma had packed in my saddlebag. I'd surely get home eventually, but God had other plans.

———

BEFORE I'D DEPARTED on my vision quest, I'd overheard Pa talking about how President Grant had made a decision to rid the frontier of any threat posed by Indians. I had feelings as mixed as my half-White and half-Comanche blood that flowed in my veins. I understood the need for ever-westward expansion by Whites, but also understood how both Whites and Indians had repeatedly violated treaties. For all the noble ways attributed to the Indian, their culture was haunted by their past. While Pa deeply respected the Red man, he described their lives as being of some far-off age that he referred to as the Stone Age. Grant had placed famed General William Tecumseh Sherman in charge of cleaning up the Indian threat. Last year, a General Ranald Mackenzie of the 4th US Cavalry defeated Kotsoteka and Quahadi Comanche at the Battle of Blanco Canyon and Battle of the North Fork. It was the beginning of the end for the proud Comanche. I'd seen the beginnings after the death of my grandfather Buffalo Hump when my uncle Spirit Talker led the remaining Penateka Comanche to the Oklahoma Territory.

I'd had no time to learn of General Sherman, but I understood that Grant had picked the right man for the job. Sherman had been responsible for the scorched-earth march to the sea that sealed the fate of the Confederacy. I wondered whether I might ever meet with him.

———

I'D LISTENED with rapt attention to stories told by Pa, Spirit Talker, and our hands about the lands to the north. I craved a chance to meet Pa's friend and my twin brother's namesake, George Freeman. Taabe seemed to be of a similar mind, as he led the way northward.

The countryside was initially quite familiar, as I'd accompanied my folks along the Pinta Trail on our way to Fredericksburg. Whatever initial trepidation I might have had about venturing out alone gradually gave way to confidence. I knew not to let confidence overwhelm good sense, as I remained ever-alert to my surroundings.

God's purposes wrapped in some sort of adventure

surely lay ahead for me. Dreams of my future were soon enough overtaken by pangs of hunger. I must provide for myself. The pemmican and jerky were only good for a few days, and I had weeks of travel ahead in reaching George's ranch.

NINETEEN
ENCOUNTERS

AS I WADED Paint across the Pedernales River, I gave brief thought to visiting the McGregors or even Reggie Wilson. I decided that if I was to be my own person, I needed to form new friendships outside the circle wrought by my folks. There'd surely be another time to visit them. I rode on.

Coming upon one of the creeks that fed the Llano River a couple of days north of Fredericksburg, I paused to water Paint. For whatever reason, I stared at my reflection in the rippling waters. While looking at my identical twin brother gave me a sense of my appearance, there is nothing like a mirror to share the truth. I was what White folks called a strapping young man. Despite or perhaps because of my mixed heritage, my skin was white and eyes blue, but my hair was raven black. I braided it in a long strand down my back. Given that I stood roughly three inches over six feet, it was a long braid. I'm not certain how long I stood with one hand on Paint's withers pondering the image reflected back at me in the waters, but the crack of a fallen tree branch startled me to the here and now.

I spun toward the direction of the sound and found myself face-to-face with the yellow eyes and fearsome fangs of one of Taabe's forest competitors. The mountain lion was no more than fifty feet away, eyes riveted on me, ears laid back, and tail twitching. All that held him at bay was Taabe's presence, as I doubted that he especially feared me or Paint. I sensed that the *pia wa'óo*, that's what the Comanche called him, was making up his mind as to whether to attack. My beautiful Spencer rifle was out of reach. I had my Bowie knife in its sheath at my rear and Colt revolver on my hip. I reckoned that *pia wa'óo* was capable of closing the gap between us in the blink of an eye, far faster than I was capable of drawing and firing.

Taabe stood rigidly alert with fangs bared. If he could talk, he'd undoubtedly be telling the mountain lion to get lost. Unlike Zeb, Taabe had no pack to call upon for reinforcements. However, I realized that he was the distraction I needed. While the stare-down proceeded, I slowly drew my gun. I had no need to kill *pia wa'óo*. I didn't need his hide nor his teeth or claws for decoration. His meat wasn't the best eating. The click as I pulled back the hammer broke the trance between wolf and lion. I pulled the trigger. The explosion from the muzzle and the bullet whizzing over the mountain lion's head sent him scurrying away as fast as his paws could propel him. I took a deep breath and holstered my Colt. Taabe seemed to duplicate my sigh of relief. Still, we'd have to be alert for the big cat's possible return. Where there was one, others surely lurked.

The encounter with the mountain lion did make me more conscious of my surroundings. I could afford no further lapses such as contemplating my reflection in the waters of a stream. I had a long path ahead of me and would surely face my share of rattlesnakes, coyotes, bears, and more. This was all very much a vast, wide-open frontier.

I alternately walked and rode. When you're on the prairies you treat your horse with much of the same care as you would yourself. Paint was a sturdy cayuse, tracing his lineage to the wild mustang progeny of the plains. He was perfect for whatever challenges lay ahead. It seemed that, with Paint, Taabe, and the teachings of my folks, God had equipped me for this trail upon which I'd embarked.

I GOT to considering that while the mid-August weather was warm here in northern Texas, autumn wasn't that far off. I'd do well to reach George Freeman's ranch by September. I was about ten days into my journey, had waded across what I figured was the Brazos River, and stopped to rest our little troop. Off to my left, among the switchgrass and mesquite, stood a young buck. He'd apparently seen me and was deciding what to do next. I think Taabe's stare might have hypnotized him. Not knowing who might be in earshot, I decided that the buck wasn't worth risking a shot from my Spencer rifle. I ever-so-slowly brought up my bow and nocked an arrow. I drew back the bowstring, aimed, and let fly. My aim was true, and the young buck instantly dropped to his knees and moments later rolled onto his side. I cautiously walked to him. He was barely clinging to life, but my knife to his throat relieved him of his death agonies. I made short work of field dressing and took the hide as well as the meat. Looking around, I reckoned this was as good a place as any to take a couple of days and rough-tan the hide while enjoying mouth-watering venison steaks. I kept my fires small so as to minimize any smoke that might attract unwanted visitors.

As to tanning, time was of the essence. I didn't figure to linger for the couple of weeks normally entailed in the process. I washed the hide in a nearby stream, scraped the remaining flesh from it, and stretched it wide, using stakes cut from mesquite branches. I used the brains from the deer for a soaking solution before stretching the skin out to dry. Over the next couple of days, I kneaded the hide to attain an acceptable suppleness. I was trying to accomplish in five or six days what normally might take more than two weeks. As a final step, I smoked the buckskin to preserve my work as best I could.

I didn't waste away from hunger during this process, as a doe fell victim to my now unerring archery skills. I had yet to tire of venison, though I filled some time drying strips to make jerky. Drying the meat in the hot, humidity-free air of the Texas Panhandle made the process easy.

The encounter with the mountain lion remained indelibly imprinted in my thinking, so I remained ever-alert to my surroundings. Taabe was my near-constant sentry, though Paint's erect ears and low nickering warnings caught my attention a couple of times. I learned that my tough-bred stallion wasn't especially fond of prairie dogs.

It was with satisfaction that I finally rolled up the buckskin, stowed the venison jerky, and resumed my northward journey. Shucks, I wasn't even out of Texas yet. I veered a tad northwest, figuring to pass through the huge Palo Duro Canyon that my pa had described.

AS I ENTERED my twentieth day since my vision quest experience, it occurred to me that I had yet to see another human. While I recognized that I was still in the Comancheria, it brought home the demise of the people of my Indian heritage. Disease, the ever-fewer buffalo, and men lost to battle had conspired to severely thin any human presence. I thought I might even spot a cavalry patrol, but that hadn't occurred either.

I finally reached what I judged to be the southern-most end of Palo Duro Canyon. It sprung up from the Prairie Dog Fork of the Red River and wound its way northwestward. There was little or no civilization ahead. Fort Elliott was far to the east and the ruins of Abobe Walls lay to the northeast. I was tracking about a hundred miles to the west of what had been popularized by Charles Goodnight's cattle drives as the Great Western Trail. The path I'd chosen was nevertheless familiar to my mind, having heard it described so often around campfires back home. Back home? I wondered from time to time what my brothers and little sister were up to. How were Pa and Ma dealing with my absence?

As I sat astride Paint, walking along the nearly dry stream bed, I found myself quite taken with the awe-inspiring vistas surrounding me. It was easy to imagine the battles and near battles my pa dealt with inside the confines of the mostly red cliffs and rock spires of the canyon. It was noticeably warmer, as the sun baked the landscape, and the canyon held the heat like one great gamut of campfire coals.

It took five days to reach the northernmost end of Palo Duro Canyon. For whatever reason—God led, I suppose—I pressed Paint onward through the hundred and fifty miles of the canyon's length. I wasn't inclined toward lingering here. Taabe happily led the way.

As I emerged from the canyon, I saw a dust cloud far to the east. There weren't enough buffalo to cause so much dust, so I reckoned it was a cattle drive. It was too far off to be sure, but I imagined drovers keeping the cattle moving, heading off strays, and keeping alert for danger.

Ahead of me lay the Canadian River, the last significant water source for a week or more. I imagined the thirsty cattle reacting to the smell of water, as they were driven into its cooling, soothing flow. I didn't envy the drovers trying to move the herd north from the river.

TWENTY
HOSTILES

BEFORE THE COMANCHE ruled the vast region known as the Comancheria, the Utes were the ruling power. They even held the mighty Navajo at bay. Like the Comanche, the Utes traced their lineage to the Shoshone tribe, but unlike my tribal kin, they'd been slow to fully understand and take advantage of the horse. Imagine my surprise when I met my first humans on this journey.

Five mounted Utes blocked my path. I'd apparently crossed paths with a frustrated hunting party. They were likely battle-tested, as word had reached as far south as Bandera of the Black Hawk War in which the Utes battled with the Mormons far to the west of where we now faced each other. In their hunt, this band was unknowingly treading on Kiowa territory. For the moment, they treaded on my territory. I wondered whether these hunters were under the leadership of Chief Antonga, who'd famously won several battles against the Mormons. They weren't very formidable-looking, as they wore no paint and were primarily armed with bows and arrows. My Spencer and Colt could make quick work of them in any fight. I didn't see any youth among them. These were older Utes like experienced in hunting, and to a lesser degree, warfare.

For now, this was a stare-down. The apparent leader looked from me to Taabe and back to me. Like my Comanche ancestors, the Utes revered the wolf. "Me Isa, *onaa* Pohya Isa of Peneteka Comanche," I finally stated with a deep, steady tone. Invoking the wolf in my name and my pa's had immediate impact. It was hard to tell whether they'd ever heard of Walks With Wolves.

The lead Ute clasped his hands across his chest in a sign of peace. "Ouray," he said, pointing to himself. "*Hoikwa tasiwoo,*" he lamented.

Ouray's name translated to arrow, and his band was seeking buffalo. I considered the still-fresh deer draped across Paint's rear. "*Ana o'a hi'it,*" I invited.

The gratefulness in the Utes' eyes were answer enough. They were hungry. They took a hesitant glance at Taabe before dismounting, but I stroked his neck and motioned them not to fear. It was still midday, and while I wasn't inclined to pause my journey, the law of the plains dictated that I join in sharing my bounty. They went to work building a fire, while I butchered the remains of the deer.

After three weeks on the trail with no human contact, I found it a relief to interact with the Utes. While our languages had grown apart in meanings and pronunciations, there were enough similarities within our Uto-Aztecan cultural roots to communicate with ease. We feasted on what remained of my deer kill, and to my relief, parted as newfound friends. Pa had advised me to strive to make allies wherever possible. He shared instances when such relations had saved his life. The Kiowa and Noconi Comanche were both examples where Pa's tough but merciful nature had forged lifelong allies.

I told the Utes that buffalo were few to the south and east. *Tosa* ranches and settlements with vast herds of cattle and horses filled the landscape. The buffalo were all but gone. Their only hope for a hunting success lay to the north. This wasn't especially well received, as they feared the Arapaho, Cheyenne, and Lakota. They were grateful for my hospitality and soon mounted up to resume their hunt. They did take my advice to the extent that they headed northwest.

I watched the Utes ride slowly into the distance. While I felt for their loss, I was filled with hope and optimism for the future. Pa had repeated Genesis 1:28 to us many times. Somewhere on the life trail before me was the opportunity to fill the earth and subdue it and reap its bounty for the benefit of His creation.

————————

THE INCIDENT with the Utes drove home the fact that I was traveling alone across a vast and dangerous frontier wilderness. Being a very social person, I was struck by the loneliness of my situation. I could sing, and I could talk, but there was no other being to converse with save the silence of the world in which I found myself. Taabe and Paint were not exactly great conversationalists.

Pa told stories of the mountain men who traveled alone and sought the vast beauty of the mountains to trap beaver and whatever other animals they could to trade for goods at an annual rendezvous. I was no mountain man, but it must have taken a special spirit to spend so much time alone in the wilderness.

I think God can have a strange sense of humor. The landscape north of Palo Duro Canyon became dryer, as I traveled through what was a great desert. Stream beds were dry and water nearly impossible to find. Pa had taught us how to conserve water, and he and Shorty had shared the locations of waterholes. However, it was Spirit Talker who taught me what natural landmarks marked the locations of water sources. Seeking hints of green plant life in the seas of browns, tans, and yellows of soil and desert flora became a regular part of my daily routine. Imagine my great joy upon finally reaching the meandering waters of the Arkansas River. I hadn't as yet resolved dealing with loneliness, but thirst would be no problem. I once again saw the dust from a cattle drive far to the east, but I wasn't able to muster the will to catch up and join them. Pa loved the cattle drive, but it wasn't in my bones.

To my west, I'd have come upon the ruins of Bents Fort. William Bent had built it back in 1833 along the Santa Fe Trail and traded with Southern Cheyenne and Arapaho for buffalo robes. He abandoned it in 1849 due to a cholera epidemic, and constructed what he named Bents New Fort near Fort Saint Vrain on the South Platte River. He eventually shuttered that trading post in 1860 as winds of possible war loomed. Bents Fort had been a welcome relief to wagon trains. It became a strategic hub of its time. The famed explorer John Frémont used Bents Fort as both a staging area and a replenishment junction for his expeditions. During the Mexican-American War in 1846, Bents Fort became a staging area for Colonel Kearny's *Army of the West*. Being intent at reaching George Freeman's ranch before cold weather arrived, I decided to explore the fort at some future time. I scanned the Santa Fe Trail to east and west, but there was nary a wagon train in sight. I pushed on.

————

CROSSING the Arkansas River marked a new stage in my journey. The countryside was still dry, but there were rolling hills, giving hints to the landscape that lay ahead. I told myself to be extra cautious, as I was entering the territory of the often-hostile Arapaho and Southern Cheyenne. There'd be Pawnee, as well, but they were at peace with the *tosas*, the Whites.

The days of travel had given me plenty of time to think about this road I'd taken. I'd left my beloved *numunahkahnis* and struck out on my own to begin a new life, one that would—God willing—endure for many years to come.

I rode Paint up from a deep arroyo cut into the soil by winter storms and found myself nearly eyeball-to-eyeball with a pronghorn. He was a beautiful specimen, his brown hide set off with white stripes beneath his horned head. The elusive and speedy pronghorn defied even the best hunters, and one had been delivered to me. I hadn't used my Spencer thus far but didn't hesitate. I drew the carbine from its scabbard, levered a round, aimed, and fired. I gave little thought to the explosion echoing among the rolling prairies as I watched the mortally wounded pronghorn fall.

I slipped from my saddle with knife in hand. There'd be pronghorn dinner this night. I began field dressing the luckless buck. I was in the midst of cutting, when I heard Paint's telltale nicker and a low warning growl from Taabe.

They had surrounded me before I could hope to react.

Encircling me were eight formidable-looking, painted, grim-faced Arapaho sitting upon their war ponies. Their stern countenances left me no room for guessing their intentions. My Spencer lay beside me, but my bow and arrows were behind Paint's saddle. I'd be lucky to get off a shot or two before the hostiles would be upon me. My mind raced. Offer them food? It was right before them, simply for the taking. They didn't need my invitation. "*Ana o'a hi'it?*" I ventured. I reckoned I had nothing to lose.

I'm sure that they were trying to make out who or what I was. I was being confronted with my half-breed status in this world. That wasn't so much a liability among the tribes, as there had been plenty of racial and tribal intermingling over many decades. They didn't share the racial prejudices of the White man, the hated *tosas*. But nevertheless, there I was, a White man inviting them to eat in the Comanche tongue, wearing buckskins, hair braided Indian fashion, and carrying the trappings of the *tosas*. Taabe was a *put-off* that likely caused them to further second-guess themselves. What sort of *sunipu* did this pronghorn killer possess that a wolf was with him? I prayed that they revered the wolf.

The Arapaho did have a long history of allying with the Comanche. I prayed that they might have had peaceful relations with the Quahadi Comanche of Quanah Parker. That could work in my favor. I knew that Chief Left Hand's Arapaho, along with Cheyenne men, women, and children under a white flag of truce, had been massacred at Sand Creek back in 1864 by a Colonel Chivington. More than two hundred Indian lives had been lost. There was certainly no love lost between them and the US Cavalry. There was a comeuppance of sorts a couple of years later, when the Arapaho joined with

Cheyenne and Lakota to entrap and wipe out eighty-one infantry and cavalry under the command of a Captain Fetterman. That event put a new perspective on what my pa reckoned would become a final great war of the plains. The Lakota chief, Red Cloud, was already forming strategic alliances, and my pa's acquaintance Tasunke Witko, known as Crazy Horse, was involved.

The apparent leader of the Arapaho band nudged his pony a few steps toward me. He was ever-wary of Taabe. He pointed to himself. "*Hosa*," he said.

From Hosa's attire, I assumed he was a chief. At that moment, I had no idea how important he was among his *numunuu*.

I pointed to myself. "Me Isa, *onaa* Pohya Isa of Peneteka Comanche," I stated with as much confidence as I could muster. Invoking the wolf in my name and my pa's had immediate impact.

Hosa looked to his warriors and gave a nod. He pointed to the pronghorn. He might have been impressed that I'd killed it, but had decided it was a worthy trade for my life. He took a long look at Paint, but shrugged. Two Arapaho warriors dismounted, hoisted the pronghorn over one of their ponies, and joined their departing chief.

I trembled involuntarily as they rode out of sight. I still had my hair, my weapons, and my horse. I was not an Arapaho victim. "Thank you, Lord," I mumbled as I mounted Paint and headed in a direction that would take me as far away as possible from the Arapaho. I would not chance them changing their minds. Taabe led the way.

———

TWICE NOW, I had encountered Indians and come away unscathed. I was either very lucky or gave off some aura, some strong *sunipu*, that resonated with them. Was God protecting me, perhaps for some greater purpose? My very name and that of my pa, coupled with Taabe's presence, certainly held impact with the Arapaho.

We reined in at a beautiful spot alongside a dried-up creek bed. I still had plenty enough water for the three of us tonight. I would need to replenish the next day, despite having two full bota bags.

Next morning, we plodded onward. Taabe always took the lead. He and I were forging an ever more intimate connection. I would call his name, and he would come to me. I began to teach him hand signals, much as I'd done with Paint but slightly more complicated. Taabe turned out to be a great student and fast learner. We could never be sure when the silent communications of hand signs might come in handy.

If Pa was accurate in his description of the trail, I reckoned I should be just about halfway to George's ranch. Despite heading ever-northward, the weather remained exceedingly warm. Blessedly, it was dryer. I understood that as our elevation headed upward, the oxygen in the air would be thinning out some. I expected that would take some getting used to.

The vista before me was dry as a bone. Somewhere within this moisture-sucking countryside was Sand Creek, the site of that massacre of Arapaho and Cheyenne. I strove to ride along the ridges such as they were of this rolling, flat landscape to enable me to see as far off as possible.

I had walked Paint for what I figured to be about an hour and had just mounted up, when I saw what appeared to be dust kicked up on the distant horizon. There were distant storm clouds and a bit of a breeze kicking up, but that dust looked to be kicked up by horses rather than the wind. The frontier is so vast that distances are often difficult to judge. It's why some folks refer to the whole panorama as *big sky*. The question growing in my mind was whether my path would intersect with the riders that were kicking up all that dust? While my curiosity was aroused as to their identity, neither was I looking to invite any kind of trouble. I tried to gauge in what direction the dust cloud moved. I urged Paint forward at a cautious walk and checked the loads in my Spencer and Colt. I wasn't seeking a fight, but I'd be ready if one presented itself.

———

IN THE SPACE of perhaps an hour, the gap between the dust cloud and me had shrunk considerably. It appeared that the riders were strung out. Now and then, the sun would reflect from polished metal, so I had begun to think the riders could be military. There were no forts close by that I was aware of. Most had been decommissioned after the end of the War Between the States. Had a decision to make. Should I engage the soldiers? After escaping peacefully from my encounters with Arapaho and Utes, logic would have it that a meeting with the US Cavalry would be no threat whatsoever. Nevertheless, I headed Paint along the side of a hillside such that I could barely see over its top. I soon determined that they were indeed a cavalry unit.

Taabe stopped and faced me with haunches up. He was warning me. Once again, I considered why a cavalry unit might be out here in the middle of a vast prairieland with no obvious ties to any source of supply. Likely as not, they were looking for Indians but had ranged farther than expected. The spirit within me told me to avoid them. Pa called it intuition, and he advised that it was best heeded. I found a thicket of mesquite in an arroyo and decided to let the cavalry pass. There was no point in tempting fate. My fifteen-year-old mind was more adult every day, as I was receiving ongoing lessons of the frontier.

Having avoided the cavalry, I headed north at a faster pace. I wanted to reach the North Platte River well before winter to afford me plenty of time to enjoy the majestic vistas my pa had described. The storm that had followed the cavalry was a blessing, as it dumped enough rain to fill small streams and catch basins along the trail from which I could keep my bota bags filled. I also managed to bag a deer, so we were far from starving. I set Taabe on the deer kill as it breathed its last, so he could enjoy the fresh kill he craved.

———

SOON, my journey brought before me the rushing waters of the South Platte River. I had begun to feel right confident that I would reach George's ranch with no further dangerous encounters. It was a mere two more weeks ahead of me. I should have known better. I think God has a sense of humor.

I reckoned to water Paint and top off my bota bags from the waters of the river. There was a stand of trees not far off that I judged to be a great spot to camp. I dismounted and led Paint toward the south bank of the river. We were perhaps fifty feet from the water when Taabe froze. He bared his fangs and let out a ferocious growl. Whatever lay ahead posed an immediate threat. I grabbed the Spencer rifle and chambered a round.

Ahead stood an immense bear. Grizzly! The very word struck fear in most any hunter, much less a lone traveler like myself. I'd heard the stories of the famed mountain man Jim Bridger battling a grizzly and his tale of survival, of encounters with grizzlies by the Lewis & Clark Expedition, and my pa and Spirit Talker twice fending off the huge beasts. The very idea of a three-inch claw raking its way through my skin sent shivers up my spine. Taabe kept growling, and that served as a distraction to the huge beast before us.

If at all possible, I preferred avoiding the grizzly. It surely wouldn't go well for either of us. The grizzly might be seriously wounded or killed, and the same possibility lurked for me. I glanced off to movement, thirty or so feet beyond the grizzly where a female and two good-sized yearlings were catching fish in the river. The male, however, was impressive for his great size. I figured him for better than a thousand pounds. Rearing up on his hind legs, he'd be better than seven feet tall. The prospect of all that bear coming at me was downright scary.

I held the Spencer such that I could quickly bring it to firing position while I slowly nudged Paint to back us away from the danger. For a moment, my efforts at peaceful resolution looked as though they might succeed. Then, one of the yearlings got curious and headed my way. The doggone sow gave a momma-style warning scream. That set papa grizzly to rise on his hind legs and split the air with a roar of his own. He stood every bit the better than seven feet I'd guessed him to be.

Taabe began to join me in backing away from engaging the bear. We ever-so-slowly grew the distance from the grizzly. The yearling moved toward us. The male grizzly wielded a great paw and slapped him back in the direction of his mama. From what I could sense, the sow remained unsatisfied with her mate's inaction toward us. He turned, arose on his hind legs again, and then dropped to all fours and charged us. I jammed the stock of the Spencer into my shoulder and fired rounds into the grizzly as fast as I could work the lever and squeeze the trigger. Froth flew from the grizzly's mouth, followed by a bloody lather. I felt his hot breath as he tumbled not more than a dozen feet from where I stood. Close! Too close! A final weak growl, a vicious gaze leveled at me, and he took his final rasping breath.

Mama bear took off with her yearlings, scolding them as she plunged through thickets along the riverbank. Hopefully, she'd live a long life and train her charges to not do what her mate had done.

Taabe tentatively approached the dead bear and took a few sniffs before gnawing into a chunk of a rear leg. Once I got my shaking under control, I checked the Spencer. I'd poured all seven rounds into the bear. "Thank you, dear Lord," I mumbled in gratitude. Now, I had a monumental task ahead. Better than a thousand pounds of grizzly lay before me. Naturally, I figured to take his furry hide and those death-dealing claws, but there was a lot of meat. I pondered how to handle so much bear. What would my pa have done? Perhaps better, what would a Comanche have done? Then, an idea struck me like a timber up the side of my head. I'd fashion a travois and drag the load behind Paint. It would slow us a bit, but that didn't matter to me, given the nature of this prize. There were decent tree limbs along the riverbank from which I could build the device. It took several hours, but I soon had my travois built and all that

I could salvage from the grizzly loaded on it. I'd been told that bear fat was an ideal lubricant and reckoned to gift plenty of bear fat to George Freeman.

———

WITH THE MORNING SUN, what remained of Fort Laramie came into view. The fort had been constructed where the Laramie River joined the North Platte. While garrisoned with Union volunteers during the War Between the States, it had been briefly abandoned and fallen into a bit of disrepair until used as a focal location for the Fort Laramie Treaty of 1868. Of course, the discovery of gold brought that treaty to the same inglorious end as the Fort Laramie Treaty of 1851. Somehow, promises made to the tribes were never kept. The teepees dotting the area around the fort were long gone, as the largesse of the government had played out. Yet, the fort stood as testament to the determination and fortitude of the men and women settling the frontier west. The local Indian Agent Thomas Twiss passed away in early 1871, and his legacy—although checkered with his occasionally erratic behaviors—would be sorely missed for his peace-keeping efforts. George, in one of his letters, noted that Twiss's wife, Mary Standing Elk, readopted her Oglala Lakota heritage and lived in Nebraska Territory.

Importantly, my arrival at Fort Laramie meant that I was less than a day's ride from George's ranch. The travois had worked out exceptionally well. However, I can't say that I enjoyed dining on bear meat. Its flavor simply didn't set well with me. I chuckled to myself upon comparing its taste to the sweet bear sign treats my ma baked. After better than two months on the trail, I still had a sense of humor. I had managed to turn ten of the bear's claws into a rather impressive necklace that now hung around my neck. I saved the others as a gift for George Freeman.

I was happy and at peace with myself. Admittedly, my mixed heritage had yet to be tested with the *numunuu* of this vast and mountainous region of the nation's frontier. The prospect of visiting with George and Running Waters and exploring the inner reaches of the North Platte country held hopes for great hunting as well as learning ever more about God's creation. I hoped to meet the Lakota that my pa had become friends with.

———

I DISMOUNTED to water Paint along the south bank of the North Platte River. I stood and breathed in the crystal-clear day with its light breeze. Carelessness, the noise from the waters of the river, the breeze, rustling leaves... blame them all. I suddenly found my arms clamped in the strong grasp of two painted warriors. In my taking in the beauty of the landscape, I'd missed Taabe's warning. Five others moved in to fully surround me. One moved to grab Paint's halter, but my beloved pinto would have none of it and bolted safely away. Taabe moved far enough away to observe.

The apparent leader stepped in front of me. He cocked his head with a curious look. It took him but an instant to figure out that I was not a White man yet was outfitted like an Indian. "Thathanka," he stated while pointing to his chest and then placing hooked fingers aside his head like a buffalo. He glared at me as if expecting a response. Given that I was half again larger than he but securely held, little wonder he could feel confident. "*Wasichus?*" asked Thathanka in apparent curiosity at my light-colored skin.

"Isa," I responded. I did my best to look over at Taabe in an effort to get Thathanka to understand that I was named for the wolf. "Penateka Comanche *numunuu,*" I added. I was determined to not panic. I had to remain strong. I struggled to recall the handful of Lakota words Pa had taught us. "Isa...tanka." I had remembered the Lakota word for wolf.

"Comanche?" Thathanka questioned. He nodded to a couple of his warriors, who promptly bound my hands behind my back and thrust a sturdy stick through my bent elbow and behind my back. It was both uncomfortable and rendered me a non-threat.

I could run but wouldn't get very far. "Comanche," I repeated and motioned my head toward the south.

Thathanka directed the tying of a long tether to my bound wrists. It looked as though I'd be doing some walking or, more likely, running.

I looked around to no avail for any sign of US Cavalry or even cowboys from area ranches.

One of the warriors struck me hard across my face.

I felt a trickle of blood run down my chin.

Another Lakota laid a serious punch into my midsection. It nearly doubled me over.

"Tasunke Witko!" I managed to blurt out in combination with a groan from the warrior's punch. In my helpless condition, I reckoned to appeal to a higher authority. I had invoked the name of the highly respected Oglala Lakota chief Crazy Horse. "Tasunke Witko *wasake,*" I repeated the chief's name and added the Lakota word for strong. "Isa *wasake sunipu,*" I said, mixing Lakota and Comanche.

"*Katá*," growled one of Tathanka's warriors. He raised his lance menacingly.

I knew that *katá* was Lakota for kill. I laid a proud, solid gaze on Tathanka. "Tasunke Witko," I invoked again. I pushed out my chest as best I could despite the pain from the punch to my stomach.

Tathanka raised his hand to stop the warrior that was insisting on killing me. There was now silence but for the fluttering tree leaves, the river, and the collective breathing of six quite fearsome-looking Oglala Lakota warriors. Tathanka was obviously considering what to do with me. "Tasunke Witko," he said almost reverently.

A seventh warrior appeared with a string of ponies. Paint would let no one come near, and Taabe was out of sight. I hoped that my wolf companion was simply waiting for an opportunity to help me. It was obvious that I would not be on horseback. Perhaps the many breaks I gave Paint by walking as we traveled northward would now pay off.

I could only hope for the best. Thus far, I hadn't been mistreated except for a couple of punches. I think Tathanka knew that hitting a defenseless prisoner was a cowardly act, though he would never accuse his warriors of that.

We headed west. I suspected that we might even pass within shouting distance of George Freeman's ranch. I tripped twice in the first mile or so, but was yanked roughly to my feet. I crossed and nearly tripped again on what I gathered were ruts from wagons traversing the Oregon Trail. Every now and then, a Lakota warrior would ride alongside me, make a threatening face at me, and even spit toward me. Blessedly, none struck me. Within the depths of my soul, silent prayers to Christ were churning.

They'd brought me what I judged to be about ten miles. Tathanka had even directed warriors to give me water twice along the way.

Tathanka stopped us at the crest of a hill and had me brought beside his pony. Down below us, the sun shone its late afternoon glow on dozens of teepees. He pointed. "Tasunke Witko," he stated firmly. I saw women with clubs and switches lined up to greet me. This was also the Comanche way of treating captives. I was about to meet my fate.

EPILOGUE

THE AMERICAN WESTERN frontier was mostly unforgiving, a meeting of savagery and civilization. The Texas Comancheria was wild country. By 1860, a few towns had begun to spring up. They served as bell-wethers to the civilizing of the frontier. *Darkness Looms: Jack Faces War* offers a peek into the courage, faith, endurance, and pure grit entailed in the conquest of the West. Life takes a new twist with the rumblings of a war among the states. It presages the decades it would take to reap the bounty the region would eventually deliver. I had to deal with man's inhumanity to man and found my own faith tested as I pursued my mission to free slaves from bondage. Importantly, I had found a purpose to strive for what was greater than myself. But in this sequel to my tale, I first face seemingly certain death. Little did I know that a great war loomed. Perhaps the greater part of my tale occurs when one of my twin sons, Isa, decides at age fifteen that it is his time to venture out on his own. Thus, 1872 becomes a pivotal year. Little did I know that the Great Plains Indian Wars loomed ahead. Another darkness or a new light?

Life expectancy on the frontier was nothing like today. A male Indian did well to live beyond age thirty, and women could expect to live a tad less. Little wonder that older tribesmen were highly respected. Life expectancy for Whites wasn't much better. A White man on the frontier tended not to live beyond his late thirties. Notably, the brevity of life generally meant that folks had to mature sooner. By the time a man or woman reached age fifteen or sixteen, he or she was pretty much an adult in terms of others expecting him or her to carry an adult set of responsibilities.

Dangers? Anthropology-minded folks claim there were as many as thirteen distinct tribes of Comanche, from the Quahadi or *antelope eaters* in the north to the Penateka or *honey eaters* in the south. Mix in Kiowa, Apache, and Tonkawa, and settlers had their hands full. The very name Comanche loosely translates in the Ute tribal language as *kumantsi* or *enemy*. Capture by the Comanche invariably led to terrible outcomes. A fearsome lot these tribes were. The horse, coupled with a long history of trade for the latest weapons and farm-grown foods in and around the Comancheria, produced a highly aggressive nomadic culture heavily dependent on the buffalo. For example, Penateka Comanche Chief Buffalo Hump led more than 600 warriors on a raid through the heart of Texas in August 1840, murdering Texans, looting the city of Victoria, and looting and burning Linnville on their march to the Gulf of Mexico. It was not until 1858 that Texas Ranger John Salmon *Rip* Ford led the force of 102 heavily armed Texas Rangers and 100 Indian allies that brought the Comanche to their knees at the Battle of Little Robe Creek on the Canadian River in Oklahoma, as depicted in a previous Frontier Chronicle *Warpath: Jack's Faith is Tested*.

The northwestern plains were peopled by many tribes but especially the Sioux, comprised of three groups: Dakota, Nakota, and Lakota. One of my previous Frontier Chronicles, *Hunted Vs. Hunted: Jack's Great Frontier Challenge* includes insights into the Lakota, which were in turn made up of seven subgroups: Oglalas (famed for Red Cloud and Crazy Horse), Hunkpapas (famed for Sitting Bull), Miniconjous, Oohenunpas (Two Kettles), Itazipacolas (Sans Arcs), Brulés (Burnt Thighs), and Sihasapas (Blackfeet). The Lakota history was no less combative than Comanche or Cheyenne. Despite the violence of the frontier, it's notable that the Lakota held to a worthy set of virtues, especially generosity, courage, fortitude, and wisdom. The North Platte country referred to in Darkness Looms: Jack Faces War was part of the Nebraska Territory that would eventually become Wyoming.

Oh, I do refer to bison as buffalo. Just for the record, bison and buffalo are quite different. Visualize the water buffalo and then the shaggy, awkward bulk of the American bison. Seems that *buffalo* came into common usage in America to refer to the bison, so I've chosen to use buffalo in my writings. Notable, too, is that the critter many unwary folks refer to as an antelope is properly called a pronghorn.

Historically notable in my Frontier Chronicles is that the longest and most used cattle trail was the Great Western Trail from 1874 to 1893. Thus, the trail I blazed in *Longhorns North* in 1857 and used in *Freedom Drovers* and *A Poison Spreads* in 1859 presaged that route, following a course roughly a hundred miles to the west of the famed Great Western Trail that ran from Mata- moros, Mexico to Val Marie, Canada. As many as three hundred thousand cattle each year would eventually be driven up that Great Western Trail.

I enjoyed no modern creature comforts. Invention of telephones was decades into the future. Transportation? Horses, mules, and oxen—ridden or pulling wagons— were the vehicles of choice. I enjoyed no refrigerator to preserve sweet treats. There were no flush toilets or showers. Folks mostly ate what grazed upon or grew from the land. Learning was squeezed from the few books that might be found, especially the Holy Bible. Can't say that the living of the era was luxurious unless you counted the sheer grandeur of majestic landscapes and of nights so quiet you could hear the stars twinkling. To fully appreciate the place, you simply had to love the incredible beauty of the outdoors. Fishing the mean- dering Guadalupe River in Texas or the chill waters of Wyoming's North Platte River, hunting deer and prong- horn, raising cattle and horses, and reaping the boun- teous yield of the rich soil was sheer joy for a courageous visionary few. For a teen on the frontier, life could be pretty good...mostly. Otherwise, it was downright dangerous.

Thus far, I had grown to manhood, conquered personal fears and prejudices, fought Indians and bandits, taken on prairie fires and storms, defended against wild beasts, traveled the wild country, driven cattle, found the love of my life, raised a family, and settled upon a life purpose. As you have seen, I especially draw upon my faith and what I was taught by my parents. And yet, all of this is constantly tested. I had to learn to trust in instincts forged from my biblical and life lessons. Yes, I'm on a frontier adventure and more. And you, dear reader, will now be able to follow in the footsteps of my son Isa O'Toole, as he seeks his own way in life and shares his adventures. May God ever bless him.

A LOOK AT: NUECES JUSTICE: LIFE, LOVE, AND LAW ON THE STRIP
(THE TUMBLEWEED SAGAS BOOK 1)

In the heart of the untamed Texas frontier lies the Nueces Strip.

It's 1856, and the once mighty Texas Rangers have been defunded, leaving a lawless land in their wake. But for Ranger Captain Luke Dunn, known to the Comanche as Ghost-Who-Rides, duty calls louder than any official mandate.

Luke's unyielding quest to bring justice to the lawbreakers of the Nueces Strip has propelled him into a deadly cycle where hunters have become the hunted. From Corpus Christi to Laredo, the land is rife with cattle thieves, ruthless murderers, and fierce Comanche warriors. And as young Elisa's heart burns with unspoken love for the stoic ranger and the vengeful Carlos Perez seeks retribution, infamy burns brighter than the Texas heat.

With a crime wave unleashed and everything converging in the small, turbulent town of Nuecestown, Texas, can Luke make a final stand for the justice he believes in—no matter the cost?

Available now

ACKNOWLEDGMENTS

Authoring books doesn't simply happen in a vacuum. The author provides the creative talent and crafts the stories, but there's so much more that demands acknowledgment. There are lots of folks and places that contribute to my authoring endeavors. So it is with *Darkness Looms: Jack Faces War*. The tale is set in 1860, transitions to 1872, and shares the trials and tribulations of a young man forced to meet the challenges inherent in the dangerous vastness of the western frontier. But this novel stands apart. At its core, it is also about the taming of that frontier. Step in two teen boys becoming men. The protagonist epitomizes the freedom of America's western frontier and represents a final bastion of honor in America. The tale follows Jack O'Toole's earlier Frontier Chronicles, beginning with adventures in *Perilous Trails: Jack's Adventure Begins*. Hopefully, readers will find *Darkness Looms: Jack Faces War* worthy of their time and emotional involvement. And then, ride into the future with Jack's oldest son, Isa.

I've been blessed with many friends and family who have supported my writings. My wife Carolyn's reviews and encouragement were a huge help, along with very important tech support from our sons Mike and Matt. Thanks to my nephew Shawn and pastor Randy for their faith insights. Many more friends and family have contributed support at some level to the creation and

publication of my Frontier Chronicles, be it encouragement or advice.

Naturally, I am major grateful to the great folks at the
Wise Wolf Books imprint of Wolfpack Publishing. The
team they bring to publishing is first-rate in editing,
cover design, and the myriad tasks that lead to successful
book sales.

It's only right to acknowledge my ancestors who were
actual settlers of the south Texas frontier. In addition to
inspiring me, they provided a quite helpful true-to-life
framework as to the life and times on the Texas Nueces
Strip. It has been appropriate to weave them into the
tapestry of my Western novels. Matthew Dunn (1815-
1855) immigrated to Corpus Christi from County
Kildare in 1845, established a homestead on Upriver
Road, and served as a sutler to General Zachary Taylor's
Army in the Mexican-American War. Peter Dunn (1807-
1890) immigrated from Ireland in 1850 and established a
blacksmith shop in Corpus Christi; John Dunn (1803-
1889), my great great-great-grandfather, raised cattle and
grew thousands of acres of cotton; Lawrence Dunn
(1837-1864) fought and died with Captain Ware's
Confederate cavalry; and my great-great-grandfather
Nicholas Dunn (1835-1912) was a rancher, drover, livestock speculator, and Comanche fighter of some repute.
My cousin John Beamond "Red John" Dunn (1851-1940)
served as a Texas Ranger in the 1870s under Captain
Bland Chamberlain (Company H), subsequently joined a
"vigilance committee," became a farmer and merchant,
and curated a museum of military weapons displayed to
this day in the Corpus Christi Museum of Science &
History. Red John Dunn's brother Matthew Dunn also
served as a Texas Ranger, and another cousin, Rut Evans,
served as a Texas Ranger in the 1890s (Company E,

Frontier Battalion, Alice, TX). My cousin Patrick Dunn was quite successful at raising longhorns on North Padre Island just east of Corpus Christi from 1883 to 1937. John Hillard Dunn (1883-1958), whose personal narrative about his family and his own adventures inspired my pursuit of my Texas family legacy, drove my own writings, and led me to write his yet-to-be-published biography *Tough Hombre—Recollections of a True Texan*. Finally, my grandfather, Horace Charles Greathouse, served as a Texas Ranger in 1920 (Company C, Austin, TX). Such real-life characters, coupled with actual events, have served to reinforce the historical settings for my writings. I've also personally walked the very landscapes traversed by my fictional and historical characters.

Most of my authoring has occurred in my office as decorated to channel my inner Texan, but my creative juices have often been inspired and imagination stoked in cafés and coffee houses across America. My favorites were Hester's Café & Coffee Bar in Corpus Christi, TX; Nueces Café in Robstown, TX; Java Ranch Espresso Bar & Café in Fredericksburg, TX; PAX Coffee & Goods in Kerrville, TX; Ragged Edge Coffee House and Bantam Coffee Roasters in Gettysburg, PA; 1889 Coffee House in Helena, MT; Dunn Brothers Coffee in Rapid City, SD; Postmasters Coffee & Bakery and Brio Coffeehouse in Waynesboro, PA; Birdie's Café and American Ice Co Café in Westminster, MD; Deja Brew Coffee House, New Oxford and Deja Brew at Miney Branch, Carroll Valley, PA; Baltimore Coffee & Tea Co., Frederick Coffee Company & Café, and Dublin Roasters in Frederick, MD; Qualle Café and Grounded Coffee & Bakery, Cherokee, NC; Palace Café, Amarillo, TX; and Unto Others Café, Lamar, CO. I must admit to also frequenting a few Dunkin Donuts and Starbucks around our fine nation.

The décors and easy-listening music in these fine establishments combined with savory cups of coffee tended to set me in the right creative frame of mind. They also afforded engagement with many fine citizens of our nation.

Last but not least, I'm especially thankful for the many folks who have read and enjoyed my books.

I do believe it's important to acknowledge how the Old West represents the brave pioneering spirit of settlers that met the challenges and transcended mere survival to enable America to achieve exceptional growth. The settling of the American frontier west is replete with tales of leveraging freedom for individual achievement. I hope you'll agree that reliving our past—even through history-based fiction—often has the effect of pointing the way to an ever-brighter future. Might we be up to it? I hope that the inspiration I've drawn from my having walked the very earth my characters have trodden, coupled with my extensive historical research, will enable readers to fully experience the grit, adventure, and passion of my characters while sensing aromas of gunsmoke, trail dust, leather, and bluebonnets.

Thanks kindly to all of you and please do enjoy *Darkness Looms: Jack Faces War.*

ABOUT THE AUTHOR

 Award-winning author Mark Greathouse's love for the western genre draws upon his deep family roots and love of the outdoors honed from teen years hiking the Appalachian Trail and family travels across America's frontier. Greathouse began writing full time after a successful career as a business executive and later as an entrepreneurial investor and advisor. His service as president of several business and community nonprofits led to their extraordinary growth. He holds a BA in English and MBA in marketing. Greathouse donates time and books annually to support wounded military warriors.

A member of Western Writers of America and the Wild West History Association, he also contributes articles on the history of America's west to western-themed magazines. Greathouse was recognized as a 2024 Finalist in western genre by the American Literary Book Awards for his sixth Tumbleweed Saga, *Nueces Truth: Texans Face War's Realities*.

His *Frontier Chronicles,* a series of western novels aimed at adventure-minded teens and young adults while weaving a Christian message within their fabric, are aimed at lighting fires of truth, faith, hope, and life purpose in the bellies of today's teen boys and girls. Just as seeds must be sown to reap the harvest, so the seeds of faith must be planted to raise tomorrow's men and women.

GLOSSARY

Bear sign—Cowboy slang for donuts.

Big Father or Great Father—All-powerful Indian deity.

Bota bag—A canteen fashioned from leather and popular among Indians, mountain men, and many travelers of the western frontier.

Cold Camp—Camp without a campfire, generally done to avoid the smoke that might alert threats.

Dog run—The sheltered space or breezeway between two sections of some southern ranch houses. Living quarters were usually on one side and sleeping quarters on the other.

Fletch—The fin-shaped bird feathers on an arrow that help stabilize its flight.

Gallery—A synonym for porch. Folks in the West often called the structures across the front of their homes galleries.

Life debt—A cultural phenomenon in which someone whose life is saved or spared by another becomes indebted or in some way connected to their savior.

Pemmican—Lean dried strips of meat pounded into a paste, mixed with fat and berries, and then pressed into small cakes.

Possibles bag (aka parfleche)—A leather or canvas sack carried by cowboys and containing essentials like soap, matches, bandages, extra spurs, smoke makings, and playing cards

Remuda—A herd of horses frequently deployed on trail drives and by Plains Indians.

Rendezvous—Annual celebratory gathering of mountain men.

Shaman—Medicine man.

Teepee—An enclosed conical transportable shelter constructed of long poles and buffalo hides with a vent at the top to permit smoke to escape.

Travois—A wedge-shaped structure constructed of two poles and a cross-beam lashed together and dragged behind horses, mules, or dogs by Plains Indians.

Comanche Translations

Aitu—Not good

Ana o'a hi'it—Phrase for *desire to eat*

Ap—Father

Aruka—Deer

Eetu—Bow

Ekakwitsubaitu—Lightning

Ekapitu—Red

Eekasahpana paraiboo—Army officer (soldier chief)

Haa—Yes

Hawokatu—Hollow, loose

Hoikwa—Hunt, look for prey

Isa—Wolf

Isa wasu—Poison

Kaahaniitu—deceive, cheat

Kahni—Life

Kamakuna—Loved one

Kee—No

Kobe—Wild horse

Kohto—Build a fire

Kooitu—Die

Kuhmabai—Married

Kuisa—Coyote

Kuuna—Fire

Kuya akatu—Afraid of

Kwakuru—Defeat someone

Kwihnai—Eagle

Mukue—Spirit

Nahuu—Knife

Natsuitu—Strong

Numu—Cow, Cattle

Numunahkahnis—Family

Numunuu—Referring to the members of the Comanche tribes. Literally: people.

Ohapitu—Yellow

Onaa—Son or daughter

Paa—Water

Pabi—Friend

Paaka—Arrow

Peeka—Kill

Pia—Mother

Pia huutsuu—Bald eagle

Pia wa'óo—Comanche words for mountain lion, puma, or cougar.

Pihi—Heart

Pohya (or **poya**)—Walk

Puuka—Horse

Sunipu—Medicine (as in strong medicine)

Suumaru—Ten

Taa Narumi—Master or God
Tabu—Coward
Tamu—Rabbit
Tasiwoo—Buffalo
Tenahpu—Man
Tomoobi—Sky
Tosa—White man or woman
Tosaabitu—White
Tumah tuyai—After life
Tuhibitu—Black
Tumhyokenu—Believe, trust
Tu Taiboo—Black man
Umaru—Rain
Unha haksi nahniaka—Phrase for *what's your name?*
Wa'ipu—Woman
Wasápe—Bear
Wutsutsuki—Rattlesnake

Lakota Translations
Ate—Father
Ayústan—Abandon, retreat, leave
Igmuwatogla—Mountain lion
Isan—Knife
Iya Tate—Wind
Iyaya—Go, leave
Jiji—Light hair
Katá—Kill
Kize—Fight
Maka—The earth and grandmother of all things
Mato—Bear
Mini—Water
Nagi—The spirit that has never been a man
Niya—Ghost
Oyate—The people or nation
Sapa—Black
Ska—White
Scan—Sky
Sunkmanitu tanka—Wolf
Takuwe—Why
Tanka—Wolf
Tatanka—The great beast (patron of health, ceremonies, provision)
Unk—Created by Maka; embodies all evil beings
Unktehi—One who kills

Wakan tanka—God (monotheistic)
Wamaka nagi—Animal spirit
Wanbli—Eagle
Wani—Four winds (weather)
Wasake—Strong
Wash tay—Good
Wasichus—White man
Wasna—Pemmican
Wi—The sun (chief of all gods)
Wica—Complete man
Wicasa—Man (gender)
Wicasa wakan—Shaman
Winyan—Woman
Wowahwa—Peace
Zuzeca—Snake

www.ingramcontent.com/pod-product-compliance
Lightning Source LLC
Chambersburg PA
CBHW011434240626
47153CB00011B/2990